The Killing Machine

Rachel Tusler

Published by Rachel Tusler, 2024.

This is a work of fiction.

THE KILLING MACHINE

First edition. May 1, 2024.

Copyright © 2024 Rachel Tusler

Written by Rachel Tusler

Cover photo by Scott Hewitt on Unsplash

Being a contract killer doesn't require you to have an extraordinary set of skills, despite what you've seen in the movies. You don't have to be a flawless marksman, proficient in hand-to-hand combat, or a master of disguises.

I mean, I imagine if you are at the elite level, flying all over the world to take out powerful crime bosses or something, that's a different matter. But the truth is, most people walk around in their lives without any expectation that they could be killed at any moment. If you're a contract killer, all you have to do is walk up and shoot them in the head.

I'm not even particularly strong—I would imagine most of the men I have taken out have more physical strength than me—and I couldn't, for example, shoot at someone accurately from a moving vehicle. But you shouldn't have to. If you find yourself getting into a physical altercation with your mark, you've likely planned things out badly.

There are of course certain things you should be familiar with. You have to know your way around a gun, and you have to learn how to stay calm through a panic. It helps if you can blend into a crowd and break into a house, and you'll do better if you have some basic knowledge about how the police operate.

But I think there are only two qualities you really need to possess to do this work: an underlying belief in your own worthlessness, and a tolerance for violence against human beings.

Once, I might have said a curiosity. Now I believe it's tolerance. If I had been a little less curious and instead simply tolerant, I might not have gotten into the situation I did.

It wasn't the usual type of job. Charlie had called Zain himself, and had told him to wait outside the girl's hotel room. He hadn't been given a dossier, though he *had* been given a weapon. But Charlie had made it very clear that all he was meant to do, for now, was to watch the girl, and to follow her if she went anywhere. Charlie had instructed Zain to call him personally and check in once a day. Before he got off the phone, Charlie had said, *Be careful. She's tough as hell, and she's unpredictable.*

Zain had driven to the hotel, which was a shithole near Redondo Beach. He had waited in the parking lot for several days, arriving early and leaving late, and had seen no sign of movement. On the third day, he had watched as a car pulled into the lot. Then Charlie got out of the car. He walked up to the girl's door, knocked, and then vanished inside.

As Zain had suspected, Charlie was somehow involved in this job. Did he have a romantic connection to the girl? It seemed unlikely that Charlie would involve Zain in his personal life. It seemed more likely that the girl was working—or had worked—for Charlie in some capacity. Charlie came out of the room a few minutes later, alone.

Early the next morning, Zain was waiting in the parking lot, and saw the door to the girl's room open. He wasn't sure what he'd been expecting, but he hadn't expected what he saw—a bone-thin woman in her early thirties with lank, chin-length brown hair, dark circles under her eyes, and dirty-looking men's clothes.

She got into her car and pulled out of the lot. Zain followed her. He followed her onto the freeway, and followed her as she drove east.

He followed her past Anaheim, past Riverside, and into scrubby desert. He followed her past Palm Springs, past Joshua Tree, and past Phoenix, Arizona. He followed through two Indian reservations, a national forest, and then into New Mexico, where stark mountains surrounded flat dry towns.

She drove fast. She stopped only at gas stations, where she went into the convenience stores and remained inside for a long time. Once, Zain went into the store after her and covertly watched her browse the aisles. She filled her basket with sodas, candy, energy drinks, packaged donuts, chips, gum, a plastic squirt gun, and a scorpion preserved in a smooth paperweight. Sometimes she would stop shopping and just stare, unblinking, at the shelves in front of her. When she reached the cashier, she bought two packs of cigarettes and a pornographic magazine, and then tossed the plastic bags into the backseat of her car without looking at them.

She did not seem to be aware of much, except maybe the tape that was playing in her own head. Zain was careful to remain out of her direct line of vision, but he thought he could have stood in front of her and stared openly and she still wouldn't have noticed him. He'd guess from the way she held herself that she was carrying—an under-arm holster, it looked like—but she had none of the wariness of a person ready to draw their weapon at any moment.

When they were outside of Las Cruces, New Mexico, just as it was starting to get dark, she pulled off the freeway. He followed her.

She drove into town and pulled up in front of a hotel that looked even shittier than the one where she stayed in LA. He watched her check in and then let herself into one of the rooms on the ground floor. She didn't seem to have a suitcase, and she left her haul of convenience store crap in the backseat of her car.

She came out a few minutes later, opened the car door, fished out a pack of cigarettes, and walked across the parking lot. Zain watched her walk into the first bar on the street. He got out of his car and followed her.

Country music was playing inside the bar, and several heads turned his way when Zain walked in. She was sitting at the end of the bar, a glass in front of her, and didn't turn when he walked up to the bar and ordered a beer. He was very aware of himself as he took his drink to one of the small tables—of his neat button-down shirt, his dark jeans, his expensive shoes, the face more than one person had called *pretty*. It was a look that allowed him to move easily in the kind of places he usually did his work. Not so much here.

He sat down and allowed himself, for one moment, to be angry. What the fuck had Charlie gotten him into? Why was he having Zain track down someone Charlie himself knew? Was this some kind of test? A trap? If something happened to the girl, would Zain be blamed? What about if she managed to slip away?

And where exactly was this headed? He followed people all the time, but he usually had some idea of where they were going, and they always at least stayed within state lines. He hadn't planned on a fucking cross-country adventure. He was lucky to have a small overnight bag in the trunk of his car, but he hadn't even watered his goddamn plants before he left.

And now he was sticking out in some hick bar, watching a mark who anyone could see was losing her shit and yet who was somehow managing to blend in in a way he couldn't hope to. If someone picked a fight with him in this place, she'd definitely notice him and that would make his job a lot harder.

He took a breath. Self-indulgence over.

He left the bar without turning around, and returned to the hotel. He got the room next to hers, then took a seat by the window and looked outside through a gap in the curtains.

Several hours later, he watched her come stumbling toward the hotel with a big, burly guy. He wore a leather jacket and had his large arm around the girl. They stumbled into the room and before long, Zain could hear the sound of a bed frame hitting against the wall.

He took out his phone and called Charlie.

Did she leave her room yet? Charlie said in his friendly voice.

She left early this morning and started driving east, Zain said. *She didn't stop driving until it got dark.*

You don't say, Charlie said. He sounded mildly surprised, but not upset. Then again, Zain had never heard Charlie sound upset. *Where are you now?* he asked.

In a hotel room next to hers in Las Cruces.

New Mexico? Charlie laughed. *Yeah, she sure can drive. How was the trip? How does she seem?*

Charlie had never asked for details about a stakeout—or not, at least, since Zain had first started working for him. Zain told him about the convenience stores, and the dead-eyed look on the girl's face.

And what's she been doing since she got to Las Cruces? Charlie asked. Zain had been dreading this question, unsure how Charlie would react to the news of the man in the leather jacket.

She went straight to the bar.

I see. And?

And she just brought a man back to her room, Zain said evenly.

Charlie laughed. *Of course she did. That poor sonofabitch.* He sounded amused. *Thank you, Zain. You did a good job. Keep at it, OK? And call me tomorrow.*

Zain hung up the phone. He could hear a kind of rhythmic rumbling sound from the room next door. Somewhat in spite of himself, he walked over to the wall and leaned his head against it.

Fuck me, he heard a woman's voice say in a kind of moan. *Fuck me, fuck me, fuck me.*

He sighed and returned to his seat by the window.

He already didn't like this job. It was one thing to follow someone in the course of their daily life. Following someone on some bleak path toward self-destruction seemed ugly. And somehow a little unfair.

. . . . .

Every day after that was the same. Every morning, he would watch her stumble from her hotel room, then head to some kind of diner, where she'd typically order coffee and several pieces of pie, only to leave it all mostly untouched.

Then she would get into her car and drive fast all day, stopping only occasionally at a rest stop or a gas station convenience store for her usual supply of sodas, junk food, and cigarettes. Her route seemed unplanned—sometimes they ended up on smaller highways, and sometimes they took long circuitous routes between towns, when another freeway would have been much faster. She drove north, then west, then circled back to head east, and then drove north again. Zain did not think she had any destination in mind—she just seemed to be driving.

She always pulled over just as it got dark. She would find the shittiest hotel in town, which was always close to the shittiest dive bar in town. She had a kind of knack for it.

He would wait in his car or his own room until she stumbled out of the bar and back to the hotel. More often than not, she'd have a guy with her—she liked big, ugly men.

And then in the morning, she'd stumble out of her room, hungover, and it would start all over again.

He would call Charlie while she was in the bar, and relate the events of the day. Charlie would only chuckle and say, *Good job, Zain. Talk tomorrow.*

• • • •

Five days after they left Los Angeles, he was sitting in his car, watching her linger outside of a diner in Indiana, seemingly unable to go inside.

The night before, she had brought two men home, and he'd heard them leave her room a few hours later, laughing and drunk. She had woken up early and headed to this diner. He'd watched her take a swig from a bottle inside her car, then get out and walk the length of the diner, peering in through the windows. But she didn't go inside.

Instead, she lit a cigarette and watched the people going in and out. She didn't glance anywhere in Zain's direction, but every so often, she would peer inside the diner at the pie they had set out on the counter under a glass dome.

She wanted to go inside, he was sure of that, but didn't seem able to bring herself to do it. She would finish a cigarette, and then immediately light another one. She watched as the waitresses cut off slices of the pie, and he saw her get more and more fidgety as the size of the pie diminished. Finally, there was only one slice left.

She put out her cigarette, but instead of going inside, she walked away from the diner, back into her car, and started rummaging through the bags in the backseat.

As she did, he watched as one of the waitresses took the glass dome off the pie, put the final slice onto a plate, and brought it to a customer.

He watched the girl locate a pack of cigarettes in the backseat of the car, then take another swig from the bottle. She seemed to be steeling herself. She got out of the car, and walked straight into the diner. She took a seat. She said something to the waitress, and then they both looked over at the empty pie plate under the glass dome.

He watched the girl's face go blank. She said something to the waitress, who shrugged and then walked away.

For some reason, he didn't want to look at the girl, but he forced himself to. She fidgeted with her pack of cigarettes, then pressed her fist against her lips. She shook her head. And then she started to cry.

It was the silliest thing he'd ever seen—a girl sitting alone in a diner, crying over a piece of pie. So why did it make him feel so goddamn lousy?

. . . .

She drove all day—headed northwest—until she finally pulled off the freeway at a small town in Minnesota. She got a room on the second floor of a run-down hotel, then headed to the bar next door.

He went to the lobby and got himself a room a few doors down from hers. When he opened the door to the room, he sighed. Fraying carpet, stained bedcover. Why couldn't she ever stay in a decent hotel?

He made his call to Charlie, then turned on the TV. A few hours later, he watched her return to the hotel with a big biker type. He set an early alarm, then went to bed.

. . . .

He woke up to the sound of a gunshot. He sat up in bed, immediately alert. He waited, but no second shot came. He took his gun from the nightstand and walked to the window. There was no sign of movement outside. No one in the hotel seemed to be stirring either.

People didn't always react when there was a single shot—it was easy to think you'd imagined it. But Zain knew what he'd heard, and had a good guess to where it had come from.

He dressed quickly, then slipped out the door. He slowly approached her room, gun drawn. The curtains were closed and the lights were out.

He walked past her door, to the end of the row of rooms, where there was a little alcove for the ice and soda machines. He stepped into the shadows and waited. Nothing happened. He knew it was possible the gunshot had been the sound of her suicide, but there had been two people in that room a few hours ago, and he wasn't ready to force his way in yet. He holstered his weapon and continued to wait.

After nearly two hours, he saw a light turn on from under her curtains. He slowly approached until he was just outside her door. He could hear someone moving around inside. Then he heard the shower turn on.

He crept back into the alcove. A little while later, the door opened and the girl stepped outside. Her hair was damp and she looked tense. She let the door close behind her. Then she reached into her leather jacket and pulled out a pack of cigarettes—not her brand, he noted.

She tried to light one, but her hands were shaking too hard to strike a match. She tried again and failed. He stepped out of the alcove and walked toward her. She tried to strike the match again, and failed again.

He didn't know he was going to do it before he did it. He stepped up to her and lit his Zippo.

Need a light? he said.

She nearly jumped out of her skin. Her hand moved toward her gun but she didn't pull it out. She just stared at him, her eyes wide.

Need a light? he repeated.

She blinked. She looked him over, and he saw her relax, just slightly. She moved her hand, which still held the cigarette, away from the gun and up to her lips. Then she leaned forward and touched her cigarette to the flame of his lighter. She sucked it to life, and then slowly blew out a stream of smoke.

Thanks, she said, and flashed her teeth in a grin. There was, amazingly, a slight dip of flirtation in her voice.

She turned around and walked down the stairs.

In a flash, Zain turned and picked the lock to her hotel room.

He smelled the blood before he saw it. The biker's naked body, a hole in his head. Stomach split open, the insides spilling out. A mess of body parts he didn't want to see spread out on the bedcover. Zain shut the door.

He quickly grabbed his things from his room, then hurried down to the parking lot. He saw, with alarm, that her car was gone. But after driving down the main road for a few minutes, he spotted her vehicle in the parking lot of an all-night convenience store. He pulled into the lot. He could see her shopping inside the store. He knew she'd take her time.

He would have to consider why he had revealed himself like that. Did he just want her to see him? If so, that was a rookie move. He filed the thought away, then took out his phone. The girl was slowly filling her shopping basket with items from the store.

Zain looked at his phone—it was 3:47am. He called Charlie's number.

What happened? Charlie said immediately.

Zain told him about the biker in the hotel room.

Charlie sighed. *Well, I can't say I didn't know it was coming. Please take care of her, Zain. Do it quickly if you can,* he said, and then hung up.

Zain had a suspicion that the girl did—or used to do—the same kind of work he did for Charlie. So why had she done what she did to the guy in the hotel room? It didn't make sense.

She came outside with two bags full of items, which she dumped in the backseat, on top of the bags that were already there. He followed her onto the freeway. Once she'd driven all day and pulled over for the night, he'd follow her into her hotel room, before she had a chance to head to the bar. He'd take her out quickly, and then he'd return to LA.

He stared into the red tail lights of her vehicle. He was glad this job was almost over.

Eighteen Months Earlier

REESE

I had a Husband. We owned a house. The house was clean, bright, and unimpeachable. So was my husband. And I appeared to be the same. But I knew, deep down, I was a scabby thing—pus-filled and rotten.

When my husband went out of town on business trips I would put on a diffrent set of clothes and drive to one of a handful of seedy bars, where I would get drunk and go home with different men. I always brought a handgun with me. I was raised around guns so I know how to use them and I was, perhaps unaccountably, afraid of getting mugged.

On one of those nights, I was talking to a guy at the bar and I didn't like the feeling I got off him. A glint of cruelty. But there was another guy sitting at the end of the bar, looking at me, who had a more appealing face.

When the first guy got up to go to the bathroom, I approached the second guy and in a minute, we were leaving together.

But we were stopped on the street by the first guy, who came after us, yelling and furious.

He was yelling at me, he was yelling at the second guy. He grabbed my upper arm. I looked down at his big fingers wrapped around my arm, and the way my flesh bulged out from under the fingers. There would be bruises on my arm the next day, I knew.

The second guy grabbed the first guy, releasing me. They started to fight in the way men do: the homoerotic shuffle, where two big bodies move one agonized inch at a time as both try to get a better grip on the other. Any punches thrown are muted and contained. I slowly took out my gun—I carried a Glock 17 at the time—and released the safety. I curled my finger around the trigger.

Finally, the first guy managed to pull out of the embrace and hit the second guy in the jaw, hard. The second guy toppled over. Then the first guy turned and lunged at me, and I shot him. He fell.

I stepped forward to look. The guy's eyes were open and yet he was clearly dead. There was a perfect round hole in his forehead. I wanted to reach down and stick my finger into that hole. I wondered if it was hot.

Back at home, I vomited profusely into the toilet. I washed all my clothes and cleaned my gun. I sat naked in the bathtub under the running shower water for hours, long after the water had gone cold.

All that night, and in the days that followed, I waited to see if the police would come. I wasn't sure but didn't think my gun, which was registered to me, could be traced off the bullet alone. But the bartender and the second guy had both seen my face. Still, I had paid for my drink in cash and there was nothing about my face or clothes that was particularly unique. But then I would wonder if there was any chance a camera somewhere had captured me—or worse, the image of my car and license plate number. Had I left behind a trail of breadcrumbs leading back to me?

• • • •

Three days after I killed the guy, Charlie came to my door. When I heard the knock, I was of course afraid it was the police, but I opened the door to a friendly-looking man in his late fifties. He was dressed in khakis and a tucked-in polo shirt. He had brown eyes and thick brown news anchor hair and a trim figure. He looked like someone's dad.

Hello there, he said warmly. *You must be Reese Thompson.*

I nodded, a little.

You can call me Charlie, he said. *I wanted to talk with you about what happened outside McGinty's bar on Thursday night. Can I come in?*

I felt all my organs collapsing into my stomach. I stood aside to let him in. He glanced around the living room, then took a seat on the sofa. I sat in one of the chairs facing the sofa. I was wearing a white dress, of all things.

The man you killed, Charlie said casually. *His name was Bud Lander. I don't suppose you knew that?*

I just stared at him. I knew he couldn't be a cop. How had he found me?

No, I didn't think so, he said. *A fellow who works for me was following Bud Lander. As a matter of fact, he was going to kill Bud Lander. Until you saved him the trouble.*

Genial, that's the word I'd have used to describe Charlie. My hands were sweating.

Tell me, Miss Thompson, he said. *Why did you decide to shoot Bud Lander at the exact moment you did? Why didn't you shoot him when he first grabbed you? Or wait longer, to see how things played out?*

There didn't seem any point denying what I had done, since he clearly knew all about it already. *I didn't shoot him any sooner because I was waiting to see what would happen,* I said. *The second guy—the other guy there—he might have won that fight. Then we could have just left. And I didn't wait any longer than I did because the first guy—Bud Lander—was coming at me. I knew it would be harder to get a good shot once he was dragging me away or whatever.*

Mmm-hmm. I heard you handled yourself very well, Charlie said, nodding. *But tell me, why didn't you kill the second man?*

The question unsettled me. It seemed like the wrong question. It also made me wonder if I had made a mistake. *Killing the first guy was self-defense,* I said. I had been saying the phrase *self-defense* to myself nonstop the past few days, but the words tasted chalky in my mouth.

Charlie's eyebrows lifted. *So it was, what...your conscience that stopped you from shooting the second man?*

It just didn't occur to me, I said, honestly.

I see. Well, that's been taken care of, Charlie said. *You'll know for next time.* Then he winked at me.

Next time? I said.

Miss Thompson, I'd like you to come and work for me.

Then Charlie told me about his business, about the types of jobs I would be doing, and how much I would be getting paid, which was a lot. He told me I'd live in Los Angeles, but I'd travel all over the country.

But I have a husband, I said. *And a house.*

Charlie looked over at the decorative glass jars I had arranged on an end table. He lightly ran his finger down the side of the glass. He smirked. Somehow, he knew I was a scab.

He looked back at me. *You were made for this work*, he said. It was a very effective thing to say. I had never felt I was made for anything. The way he said it, it acknowledged that even though I was a scab, there were some things scabs were useful for.

He stood up and walked to my front door. He picked up an envelope out of the little bowl we used to collect mail. The envelope contained some kind of bill. Charlie took out a pen and wrote a phone number on the envelope, then handed it to me.

When you're ready, he said, *call this number.*

My husband was returning home the next day. I woke up early and did some laundry. I made chocolate chip cookies and put them out on a plate in the kitchen. I snipped three pale blue hydrangeas off the bush in the backyard, and arranged them in a small rectangular vase, which I put on the coffee table.

I sat at the kitchen table, staring at the cookies. And then I picked up the phone and called Charlie. He gave me an address in Los Angeles. I went to the bedroom and changed into jeans, a t-shirt, a leather jacket, and boots. I slid my gun into the waistband of my jeans.

I grabbed my car keys. I left everything else behind.

• • • •

For six weeks, I stayed in a house that Charlie owned in Culver City. I spent a lot of time with Cliff who, it turned out, was the guy who had watched me kill Bud Lander. Cliff was a tall, muscular white guy with very short gray hair. He was a former Detective with the LAPD who hated the LAPD. Cliff took me to the shooting range every day, bought me a bulletproof vest and a gun harness, and taught me about how cops think.

I learned other things, too—a Taiwanese guy called Jay taught me how to break into and hotwire cars, and we drove all over the city together, honing my driving skills. Another guy—a quiet older man who Cliff just called The Locksmith—showed me how to pick a variety of locks. He also drove me through different neighborhoods, and stopped in front of random houses to explain the most likely security flaws of each, and the best ways to break into them.

When I had first arrived at the house in Culver City, Charlie had taken my car keys, my gun, and my ID, and had promised he'd replace it all. About two weeks into my training, Charlie showed up at the house with a new passport under the unlikely name of *Jessica Carter*. I got a new driver's license and set up a bank account under the alias—Cliff explained to me that we were lucky that Charlie paid us directly into a bank account, instead of using cash.

Cliff also took me to the mall and bought me two new mobile phones. The first was a non-smartphone and was to be used for one thing only—to receive incoming calls about my next job. I mentally dubbed it The Charlie Phone. The other phone, a smartphone, was for everything else. I would use only burner SIM cards with it, and I'd replace the SIM cards before and after every job.

Not long after I got my new driver's license, Cliff showed up at the house in a new silver Ford Fusion, and handed me the keys. I knew the Fusion handled all right, but it had a weaker base engine than I liked in a vehicle. Still, I tried to look grateful. Cliff had told me it was a gift from Charlie.

Every few days, Charlie would come over to the house and talk to Cliff about me, and then we'd sit in the living room and drink iced tea and he'd talk to me about the work.

Cliff tells me you're a quick learner, he said once. *And a good shot. He thinks you'll be ready for your first job soon.*

Why not now? I said.

Charlie laughed. *Why so eager, kid?*

I shrugged. *That first time, it happened so fast. This time, I wanna really see what it's like.*

Charlie looked at me for a second. *Wanting to know things isn't bad,* he said. *But you have to be careful. The most important thing I can tell you is that the act itself should happen fast. Cliff will tell you more about what that looks like in practice. But what you should also know is, doing it fast like that may make you get a kind of itchy feeling. Like you want to experience the whole thing more fully. Like you want to experience some kind of, let's say, communion. But you always have to remember this—don't ever get too close to the work.*

OK, I said, though I wasn't sure I fully understood.

That's true even when the job is done, Charlie said. *Sometimes, for example, people's insides will be on the outside. You might feel the urge to look more closely. Don't. Looking too close at that kind of thing can get a person in a bad way. I've seen it more than once.*

I didn't say anything. I had never seen anyone's insides on the outside, so I wasn't sure how I'd react. I remembered my desire to stick my finger into the gunshot wound in Bud Lander's head. I wondered if Cliff had seen my hesitation as I stared over the body and guessed what it meant.

Cliff taught me about fingerprints and DNA. The good news, he told me, was that none of my information was on file in the FBI database. That meant if I left a fingerprint on a crime scene, they couldn't trace it back to me. Still, I had to be careful. I didn't want to create a link between the crime scenes, especially with something as unique as fingerprints. During the hit, I would be wearing gloves at all times. Though it wouldn't be ruinous if I left a hair behind, it would be a good idea to wear my hair in a ponytail, Cliff said. Or cut it shorter.

The next day, I took a pair of scissors and hacked my hair off at the chin. When Charlie came by that afternoon, he looked at me and said, *Jesus Christ. Get in the car, kid.*

He took me to a barber to get my hair evened out. *You want to look inconspicuous, not like a goddamn nutjob*, he said. *Along those lines, can we maybe get you at least one change of clothes?*

I had been wearing the same outfit since I left home, weeks earlier. Charlie took me to the Macy's at the mall and I picked out two pairs of jeans, seven white t-shirts, seven pairs of underwear, seven pairs of black socks, and two bras. Charlie paid for it all.

Afterward, we went to the 1950's style diner just off the food court. We sat in a booth with shiny red vinyl seats. Charlie got a root beer and I got a hot fudge brownie sundae—which consisted of a warm brownie topped with two scoops of vanilla ice cream, whipped cream, hot fudge sauce, chopped peanuts, and a maraschino cherry.

Hey, he said, *I've got a question for you. Do you ever think about Bud Lander?*

I thought about the round hole in his forehead. *Sometimes*, I said.

What do you think about?

I think about how his face looked after he died, I said.

Ok, Charlie said nodding. *Do you ever think about, say, his family? What kind of guy he was?*

No, I said.

What about the other guy, the one you left the bar with?

You said he was taken care of, I said.

He was. But do you ever think about him, about why he had to die?

I dipped my spoon into the dish, and wedged it into the brownie. *No*, I said.

Do you ever think about your husband?

I pushed my spoon the rest of the way through the brownie, cutting off a piece, then scooped up a dollop of ice cream streaked with hot fudge sauce, and a few chopped peanuts. *No*, I said, then popped the bite into my mouth.

Ok, Charlie said. *Good. In a few days, you and Cliff are gonna go on your first job.*

Really? I said, feeling a kind of tingling spreading all over me.

Really, Charlie said, smiling.

Who is it?

Cliff will tell you all about it. He'll arrange the travel, and he'll walk you through everything. In the meantime, you might wanna think about finding a place to live. Somewhere to be your home base when you're in town.

Sure, I said. I was still thinking about the first job. Finally, things were going to *begin*.

If you need, I can front you some money for the deposit, Charlie said. *And Cliff can tell you what neighborhoods you might wanna look at.*

That's OK, I said, *I'll figure it out*. I still had a little cash. And I didn't care where I lived.

Suit yourself, Charlie said. *And do me a favor, kid,* he added. *Eat a vegetable some time.*

I stuck my finger into the whipped cream, scooped up a mound of it, and licked my finger clean.

• • • •

That afternoon, I got in the Ford Fusion and drove around for a little while. Eventually, I pulled into the parking lot of a run-down single-story motel. It was in an L-shape, with all the doors facing the parking lot. Easy to get in and out of. Nothing fancy. The rooms were $42 a night. I paid in cash for a smoking room on the ground level. It had a minifridge and bars on the window. That seemed just right.

A few days later, Cliff and I were on a plane to Chicago. I had only been on a plane a few times in my life, and that was when I was a kid. I had to resist the urge to fiddle with the tray table, the seat adjuster, and the glossy safety pamphlets.

Do you always fly to the job? I asked Cliff.

Pretty much, Cliff said. *Of course, after this one, you'll go on your own.*

If I don't screw it up, I thought.

The flight attendants were approaching with their rolling cart. *Can I get a drink?* I asked Cliff.

Do what you like, Cliff said. *We won't start the stakeout until tomorrow.*

The stakeout. I loved the sound of that. I ordered a rum and coke from the flight attendants. The sickly sweet, dirty taste of it thrilled me.

Have you ever been to Chicago? I asked.

Will you stop messing with the tray table? Cliff said. *Yes, I've been to Chicago. Great town.*

We're probably not gonna see a lot of sights, though, huh? I said.

No, Cliff said, and sighed. *We're not going to see a lot of sights.*

Do you know anything about this job? I asked.

No, he said. *You never fly with any of that information on you. You'll find out what you need to know once you arrive at your destination.*

At the airport, I saw a bright red and yellow sign for a fast-food restaurant advertising Chicago Hot Dogs. I gasped and grabbed Cliff's arm. *Can we get a Chicago Dog?*

Fine, Cliff said. *But that'll be your dinner.*

I ate two Chicago-style dogs, standing up, outside the airport rental car kiosk, while Cliff signed the paperwork for our car.

We walked through the parking lot and stopped in front of a gray Chevy SS.

I hear you know something about cars, Cliff said. *What do you think?*

Of the SS? I said. *I think it's great. Underrated. The styling sucks, but who cares? It has top horsepower with a V-8 engine and handles beautifully. Plus, it's unassuming. It's only too bad they don't make them anymore.*

Good, Cliff said, then tossed me the keys. *You can drive.*

We did the things Cliff told me I'd do before every job: we went to a shipping company and picked up a bag from one of their lockers. Then we went to a different company and picked up a manila envelope. Finally, we got a couple of burner SIM cards from a store in a strip mall.

After that, I drove us to our hotel, a Sheraton back in the direction of the airport. We were staying in adjoining rooms, but Cliff had us convene at the little table in his room. He handed me a pair of latex gloves, and I put them on while he did the same.

Cliff opened the bag we'd picked up at the first locker, and pulled out a plastic Ziploc bag with two identical-looking guns inside, plus a box of bullets, two noise suppressors, a white piece of folded cloth, and a small bottle containing clear liquid. He took out one of the guns and handed it to me. It was a Beretta APX, a gun I was familiar with.

Make sure you never touch the bullets. If you do, you have to clean them—that's what the solution is for, he said, and held up the little bottle. *Try and collect any bullet casings you drop during the hit, though if you can't find them right away, it's more important to leave the scene. After the job, you'll clean the weapon, the noise suppressor, any unused bullets, and the casings, and return it all by mail to the address we give you.*

Cliff handed me one of the noise suppressors, which I had used during our training.

This won't be like the shooting range, he said. *You might be surprised by how loud it is if you do the hit indoors.*

I screwed the black tube onto the gun while Cliff watched.

Still, the suppressor brings the decibel level down enough that a neighbor or whoever is less likely to hear it and call the cops. Plus, it'll help protect your ears in the long run.

I nodded.

Do you know you stop fidgeting when you have a gun in your hands? Cliff said. *You got any questions?*

What about the envelope we picked up? I asked.

Getting to that. Any questions about your sidearm?

At moments, I could imagine Cliff as the cop he used to be. Didn't take any guff, see. I felt the weight of the gun. Though I hadn't noticed, I wasn't surprised I'd stopped fidgeting. I felt calm with a weapon in my hands. *Will it always be a Beretta?* I asked.

No, it'll depend on the job. If there's a type of gun you like most, let me know, and I'll try and make sure that's what ends up in the bag.

A Glock 17 or 20, I said. *Or a Sig Sauer P210.*

Fine, Cliff said. *Now, the dossier.* He opened the manila envelope and pulled out a stapled sheaf of papers. *This includes whatever information we have about the mark—their name, age, address, their typical schedule, that kind of thing.*

Once the hit is done, you'll destroy this, Cliff said. He handed me the dossier, and sat while I read it over.

The mark's name was Fred Hitchens. The dossier said he was 50 years old, white, and six feet tall. In the photos, he looked unremarkable—a middle aged man with a light beard. He had a 15-year-old son named Brian and was currently separated from his wife, Dani.

He's separated, I told Cliff. *Do you think that means the wife ordered the hit?*

Listen, Cliff said. *You'll learn that there are useful questions to ask, and less useful questions. That one falls into the latter category. Don't try and figure out who's behind the hit. Frankly, it's none of our business. More importantly, trying to probe into the inner life of the mark isn't a good choice. OK?*

OK, I said.

I continued reading the dossier, which was put together like a badly-written CV. It contained a great deal of information I didn't think would be useful.

This says Fred Hitchens went to law school, made it all the way through, and then failed the bar exam and gave it up, I said. *Why do you think it includes that?*

I don't know, Cliff said. *The client just provides whatever information they think will be useful. Most of it isn't. But you gotta read through it all the same.*

But, like, why do you think the client thinks that's important? Is it supposed to tell us something about the mark, you know, psychologically? I asked.

Hey, Fidget, what kind of question do you think that is?

A less useful question? I ventured.

Bingo, Cliff said. *You can go to your room now. Bring that dossier back when you're done with it so I can give it a read. And try and get some sleep tonight. We'll get up early tomorrow, and it's gonna be a long day.*

I didn't follow Cliff's advice, of course. I was so excited I barely slept. Instead, I spent hours staring into the mirror, wearing only my underwear, pointing my gun at the glass.

• • • •

We woke up before the hotel had even started serving its buffet breakfast, but Cliff agreed to let me stop at a fast-food drive-through for breakfast sandwiches before driving to Fred Hitchens' apartment.

He lived in a suburb north of Chicago that was filled with strip malls and chain restaurants. When we reached his block, I pulled over and parked the car. His apartment building was a little further down the street—a yellowish building from the 1970's with an ugly stone facade.

We waited for Fred Hitchens to appear. It was 5:45am.

Most of the job is going to be watching and waiting, Cliff said. *You're trying to get to know your mark's routine. Most people have pretty set routines, so it rarely takes long to find your opportunity. Choose circumstances you've already seen the mark in, so you'll know how he walks into a situation and how he gets out of it. And then you step right into the middle of that situation and make your move. Simple as that.*

You always plan it out before you do it? I asked. *You never just, I don't know, see an opportunity and act?*

Nine times out of ten, a spontaneous hit is the wrong hit, Cliff said. *You have no idea what might be coming. So even though it might look like a great opportunity, it's usually not worth the risk.*

What about the tenth time out of ten? I asked.

OK, sometimes your mark will go wandering down a dark alley in the middle of the night, dead drunk. An opportunity like that is too good not to take. But that's the exception. You got it?

Got it, I said.

Then comes the act itself. You never know how people are going to react. You heard of fight, flight, or freeze?

Sure, I said.

When confronted by a stranger with a gun, your mark will either try and fight you, try and run, or just freeze up. Now, freezing makes it easy on you, but the other two? You don't wanna try and chase someone down a busy street, and you definitely don't want your mark to jump you. Especially you—you're small and I'm guessing you don't have any hand-to-hand combat training you neglected to tell me about?

I shrugged.

The trick is to do it before the mark has a chance to react, Cliff continued. *Hopefully before they even see you. Practically before you even know what you're doing.*

The door to the apartment complex opened. I took a breath, but an older Black woman stepped out of the building.

Not Fred Hitchens, I said.

No, Cliff said.

What if he notices us when he comes out?

If he makes us, you mean? It happens. Especially if someone is already on edge. You get made, you gotta trade in your rental car for another one. Your mark might disappear on you for a couple days. But they always come back home. When they do, you act quickly.

A woman jogged by the car. I watch her ass wiggle in the spandex pants.

Keep in mind, though, most people are totally oblivious to the idea someone might be watching them, Cliff said. *The thing you have to worry about more is other people. A person sitting in a parked car can start attracting attention in certain neighborhoods, and you might not notice because your attention is on the mark. You've got to be especially careful when you're doing a stakeout in some quiet suburb like this, more so if it's a richer neighborhood. Move your car often. If the stakeout goes on for too long, that's another reason to swap rental cars. Don't ever try to pretend you're invisible, that doesn't work. Always know what you're pretending to be—a tourist, a girl visiting her aunt, whatever—and be prepared to be that for the cops, a nosy neighbor coming by, whatever.*

Who are we today? I asked.

My daughter and I are visiting from Phoenix for a few days, for her grandmother's 80th birthday. We're staying with my brother who lives nearby. We're sitting out here because, to be honest, we needed a little break from all the festivities.

I looked away and smiled. Ridiculously, I was happy that Cliff had cast me as his daughter in his cover story.

The door to the apartment complex opened again, and Fred Hitchens stepped outside. I'd been afraid I wouldn't recognize him, but now that I was looking at him I had no doubt.

It's him! I hissed.

It's him, Cliff agreed.

He was a big, broad-chested guy—he looked like he used to be well-muscled, but was softening to fat. He had brown hair streaked with gray and a short scruffy beard that was coming in all gray. His face looked lined, and weary. I liked the look of him.

He walked to a Jeep Cherokee parked on the street.

Get ready to follow him, Cliff said. My heart started beating fast.

Fred Hitchens pulled out and, after a minute, I did the same.

Keep a few cars distance between you, Cliff said. *In all likelihood, he's just going to work.*

I followed him onto the freeway.

Another thing to keep in mind, it's always better to lose a guy than risk him seeing you, Cliff said. *You're trying to get a sense of how he spends his days, but you don't need to know what he gets up to every second. You know where he lives. If you lose him, he won't be lost for long.*

Fred Hitchens' turn signal came on. I prepared to follow him.

Yep, this exit will take him to his work, Cliff said.

I was a little disappointed. I was hoping for some kind of a surprise.

He pulled into the parking garage of his office building, and we circled the block. After about ten minutes had passed, we entered the garage. We located the unoccupied Jeep Cherokee and parked nearby.

And now, Cliff said, *We wait some more.*

We sat in the car for hours. Cliff told me more about cover stories, and watchful neighbors, and how to follow someone covertly. Around noon, he opened the glove box, pulled out two meal replacement bars for us, and handed me one. It was chocolate chip flavored. It had 440 calories and a long ingredient list. I chewed it slowly. It was very dry. After a moment, I realized Cliff was looking at me.

Taste like shit, don't they? he said, and sighed.

After we ate, Cliff told me to head to the gas station outside the parking garage to use the restroom. *You go first, then I'll go*, Cliff said. *An advantage to working in a team. Try not to drink too many liquids when you're on a stakeout. And I'd advise you to learn how to piss into a cup.*

Inside the gas station convenience store, I looked at the hot dogs rotating on the rack next to the cash register, and wondered why I'd had to eat the meal replacement bar.

Finally, around 6:30pm, Fred Hitchens appeared and returned to his vehicle. I followed the jeep out of the garage, and then to a closer-in suburb with nicer homes than in his neighborhood.

The wife's house, Cliff said, looking at the dossier.

They're separated, I reminded him.

Fred Hitchens pulled up in front of a newer-looking house with large front windows. He got out of the jeep and walked toward the front door. As he did, the door opened. A middle-aged woman was standing there. She had her blond hair cut into a bob and wore a lot of make-up. Her arms were tightly crossed and she was saying something. She seemed upset with Fred Hitchens. He kept putting up his hands in a gesture of innocence. Finally, the woman turned and called into the house. A skinny teenager with long brown hair slunk out the front door.

He didn't look at either of his parents, just started walking toward the Cherokee. The woman shook her head and shut the door to the house. Fred Hitchens said something to his son, who didn't even glance at him, just shrugged and climbed into the car. Fred made a kind of joking hopeless gesture to the sky, as if saying to God, *See what I put up with?*

I liked that. Fred Hitchens couldn't know that for this one moment, he actually had an audience. It gave a kind of brief grandeur to his life before he died, I thought.

We followed them to a nearby local fast-food restaurant. We parked on the other side of the parking lot from the Cherokee, then watched them walk into the restaurant.

I feel like this is the kind of separation that leads to divorce, I said. *I feel like this is an acrimonious separation.*

Cliff shushed me.

About half an hour later, they came out of the restaurant. Neither of them spoke to each other as they walked to the car. I guessed that the son hadn't spoken a word the whole time they were in the restaurant. They drove to a nearby movie theatre, and we waited in the parking lot for a few more hours, then followed Fred as he took his kid back to the mother's home. Finally, we followed him back to his apartment, where we waited just to make sure he didn't leave again.

Do you feel bad at all? I asked Cliff as we stared up at the light in what we knew was Fred Hitchens' apartment.

How do you mean? For the mark?

Yeah? Like, right at this moment, are you feeling bad?

No, Cliff said. *The world has too many people in it, anyway. We're all gonna die—he's just gonna die sooner than he planned, no doubt as a result of something he did. I don't feel a lot for people I don't know.* Cliff shrugged. *That's caused me some problems in my life, but it makes me good at my job now. How about you? Do you feel bad?*

No, I said. *I feel impatient. But I don't feel bad at all. Maybe that means I'll be good at the job?*

Let's wait and see once it's over. You never know how you're gonna feel about it until you do it.

OK, I said. *Can I ask you something else?*

Sure.

Do you have, like, a normal life? When you're not working, I mean?

Is that what you want? A normal life?

I thought of the cool, clean house I shared with the Husband. *No, I said. I guess I was just curious.*

Sure, most people would say I have a normal life. I have a family who thinks I travel for work a lot, which isn't even really a lie. I get to spend a lot more time with them than I did when I was a cop. We've got a real nice house.

I nodded.

I'll tell you, something, though, Fidge, cuz I like you and because, honestly, you seem just a little less than stable. I'm different now. Most people can't tell. My wife, she's the only one who's ever said anything. She thinks I'm having affairs. We used to fight about it, but now she's reconciled herself to it, because I'm calmer and easier to be around and can pay for our kids to go to fancy colleges.

I nodded again, thrilled to get some personal information from Cliff and trying not to show it.

All I'm saying, Cliff said, *Is that doing this work changes you. And you should be prepared for that. You'll never again be the person you are right now.*

That didn't sound so bad to me.

• • • •

In the morning, we followed Fred Hitchens when he left his house. This time, he got off at a different exit, and pulled into the parking lot of a large office building.

We parked the car.

What kind of office do you think this is? I asked.

Couldn't say, Cliff said.

I looked at the placard near the entrance. Almost every business was two names connected by an ampersand: Sanders & Gregg, Lew & Hoffman.

I think they're mostly lawyers, I said. I pulled out my phone and Googled the first one on the list.

Listen to this! I cried. *Chicago Divorce Lawyers for Men! I knew it!*

Less useful questions, Fidge, Cliff said in a warning voice.

I put away my phone.

A few hours later, Fred Hitchens returned to his car and I followed him, at a discreet distance, to his work, where he parked in the garage.

We waited in the parking garage all day again, getting out of the car only to use the restroom at the gas station, where I bought us each two hot dogs, plus potato chips, packaged donuts, and a couple of energy drinks, which Cliff refused to drink. Finally, Fred Hitchens reappeared around 5:30, and I followed him out of the garage. I followed him onto the freeway—headed south, this time—for a few exits, then into a kind of middle-class Chicago neighborhood that was mostly made up of two-story brick apartment buildings. Fred Hitchens parked in front of one of the buildings. Cliff had me drive past him—a good strategy, he said, to allay any possible suspicions—circle around the block, then return to park a few houses down the block from Fred Hitchens' jeep, which was now unoccupied.

After a few minutes, the door to the building opened. Fred Hitchens came outside with a young woman who was holding a small dog. She had long dark hair and was wearing yoga pants and a tank top. The dog was some kind of long haired chihuahua. The woman was talking to Fred Hitchens and gesturing at the dog. She looked irritated. He kept nodding his head.

Do you think that's his girlfriend? I asked.

Probably, Cliff said.

She wasn't in the dossier, I said. *How old do you think she is?*

Late twenties? Cliff said.

Younger than me, I said. *Do you think all the women in his life are mad at him?*

Maybe so, Cliff said.

She handed the dog to Fred Hitchens. He set it down, and they started to walk down the block.

It must be the wife who hired us, I said.

You ready to listen to me, Fidge? Cliff said.

Yeah, I said, suddenly nervous.

The idea is you follow the mark until you get a sense of their schedule and their habits. More than anything, you start to learn their rhythms. You understand when they're on guard and when they're not. You understand how they behave when they think they're alone. But don't ever imagine that you know what's in their souls. You'll drive yourself crazy if you start thinking that way.

You sound like Charlie, I said. *He told me not to get too close to things.*

Charlie's not wrong. I've been at this job for a long time, and I've stayed sane cuz I keep a tight rein on my mind, Cliff said.

Do you think I can do that?

I don't know, Fidge. You've got a roaming all over the place kind of mind, I think.

Yeah, I said. I had thought Cliff was letting me run my mouth because he was getting tolerant of my curiosity. But now I realized he was waiting to see if I would acquire some self-control. Which I had entirely failed to do. I was suddenly afraid I wasn't cut out for the job after all.

We watched Fred Hitchens and his girlfriend return from their walk. He was carrying a little green plastic bag of dog shit. We waited outside the girlfriend's house for several hours, then followed him when he left, close to midnight. We watched him take the exit toward his house, but didn't bother following him home.

We won't do an early stakeout tomorrow, Cliff said when we returned. *Let's meet for breakfast in the hotel lobby at seven.*

Is everything ok? I asked, suddenly afraid that Cliff had decided to kick me off the job.

Cheer up, he said, clapping me on the shoulder. *We're gonna make a plan.*

• • • •

I filled my plate at the buffet breakfast, then joined Cliff at a table, where he was eating bran flakes.

OK, pretend you're here on your own. Cliff said. *Today's Thursday. That means you have to do it today or tomorrow. You rarely wanna kill anyone on a weekend—people change their routines on a weekend. So, what are you gonna do?*

Well, I don't want to take him out at home, I said.

Why not?

The door to the apartment building is locked, I said. *I could make up some story and follow one of his neighbors in, but then someone would see me, and I don't like the idea of having to get out of the building after I do it.*

Good call, Cliff said. *I like taking people out on the thresholds to their homes. It works well for houses and even hotel rooms, if there aren't any cameras. But not apartment complexes. There aren't enough exits and there are too many residents around. So what are you thinking?*

Maybe the parking lot at his work? I said.

Go on.

I could follow him tomorrow and...take him out when he gets out of his car?

Or you could go down there today and do it as he's getting into his car, Cliff said.

Today? I repeated.

Why not? There aren't any cameras in that garage. You know what his car looks like. You can park near it and just watch and wait. His Jeep uses keyless entry but he'll still take a moment to stand there and tap the button. Moments of distraction are the best time to act. What do you think?

It seemed like such a strange idea. Fred Hitchens was going to die today. *OK,* I said.

OK, Cliff said.

We talked through the plan step by step, until it seemed as ordinary as a trip to the bank.

What's wrong? Cliff asked as I poked at my breakfast.

Doesn't it seem a little, I don't know, bloodless?

Bloodless?

Just shooting him in the head and then leaving like that? Doesn't it seem kind of removed from what you're doing?

That's the point, Fidge. You gotta stay removed. You try and take away that remove, and you're a goner. Either you'll get arrested or you'll lose your fucking mind. Rein in your thoughts, remember?

I nodded.

Besides, no one feels too removed the first time. What you'll probably feel is abject fucking terror.

I laughed nervously.

What does it feel like when you panic? Cliff said.

When I panic? I repeated. *I guess it feels like I'm trapped,* I said.

No, I mean, what does it feel like in your body?

In my body? I hesitated. I didn't pay that much attention to my body.

Imagine you're panicking right now. Imagine that a group of cops suddenly surround this hotel, guns drawn. How would you feel?

It was easy enough to imagine. *Well, my heart would be going, and my mouth would be dry. I'd sweat—my hands and armpits especially.* Just thinking about it made my palms damp. *My stomach would get tight. And I'd wanna run. Or shoot someone.*

Good, Cliff said. *This is panic. This is not an actual situation. Cops showing up, your mark seeing you, your weapon not working, those are all situations, but this thing happening in your body is not a situation. It's just a combination of feelings—those feelings in your chest, your stomach, your mouth. You are going to experience panic, probably on your first job. Maybe on every job. And the panic will feel like a situation, and you'll feel like you gotta do something about it. Run or shoot or whatever. But I'm telling you—and this is probably the most important piece of advice I'll ever give you—don't do anything about it. You gotta just breathe through the panic. Let the situation guide your choices, not whatever is happening in your body. What's happening in your body is good—it's telling you you're alive—but it's not what makes the decisions. Got it?*

Got it, I said.

Now stop fidgeting.

I looked at Cliff. He didn't look angry, but he looked serious. I released the napkin that was balled up in my fist, and let my hand rest open-palmed on the table. I took the other hand away from my face and set it next to the other one. And then I sat. My hands seemed to itch, wanting something to do. I felt the desire to touch something rise in my body, stronger and stronger. Still I didn't move. I felt the cool table top against my palms.

I took a breath. I realized the intense desire to move was fading, slightly, and then more and more. I breathed again. I became still.

Good, Cliff said. *Good job. Sometimes you control your mind by controlling your body.*

· · · ·

I drove to Fred Hitchens' work. I located the Jeep Cherokee in the parking lot. I parked in the space across from it. I waited.

My stomach was a black snake, coiling ever tighter into a mass of knots. I had sweat through my t-shirt. My heart beat hard in my chest. I didn't smoke. I barely moved.

At 3:00pm, I took the latex gloves Cliff had given me out of my pocket, and slipped them on. Then I removed my weapon and attached the noise suppressor, then tucked it back into my holster. I watched Fred Hitchens' car from the rearview window.

I waited. 4:00pm passed. 4:30pm. 5:00pm. Cars drove past, leaving the parking lot. I was still and taut. Perhaps *I* was the coiled black snake. Anxiety would not dictate my actions, I told myself. I would strike exactly when needed.

5:30pm passed. 6:00pm passed. 6:30pm. Questions began to rise...had I located the wrong car? Made some other mistake? I let the questions float away. I felt the hard metal of my gun press against my ribs.

I saw a movement from the corner of my eye. I turned my head and saw Fred Hitchens, walking toward his car.

I scanned the area. There was no one else in the garage. I opened my car door. Fred Hitchens was approaching from the other side, so I was shielded from view by my vehicle. I crept the length of my car, then withdrew my weapon and pulled back the slide to chamber a round.

Fred Hitchens was nearing his car. I watched him turn and walk alongside the jeep, toward the driver's seat. I stood up and walked toward him. He lifted the hand holding his key fob. I raised my gun.

Suddenly, he turned around. His eyes got big. They were surprisingly blue. He had a look of shock. He *saw* me. It sent a shiver through my body. I aimed the gun at his forehead and pulled the trigger.

There was a loud bang, and Fred Hitchens fell.

I waited for a moment. My ears were ringing. I approached the fallen man and looked down.

Blue eyes staring up blankly. A neat round hole ringed in blood. Fred Hitchens was dead.

I turned around and headed back toward my vehicle, stopping to pick up the bullet casing on the way. My heart was in my throat as I got into the car. I tore off the gloves and threw them on the passenger's seat. I drove out of the parking garage, careful not to speed even though all I wanted to do was get the fuck out of there.

In a moment, I was back at the hotel parking lot. I barely remembered the drive. My gun was in my holster, minus one bullet. I was still in one piece. I had heard no sirens. I waited a moment, just to make sure no one had followed me, then walked into the hotel.

I went straight to Cliff's room, as he'd instructed me to do.

He opened the door and quickly let me in.

Is it done? he said. It was the first time I'd ever heard anxiety in his voice.

It's done, I said. I told him what had happened in a flat-sounding voice.

I watched his face relax.

You're sure he's dead?

I'm sure, I said.

And you didn't see anyone in the garage?

No, I said.

OK, he said. *OK. Good. You've got that casing, and your piece?*

I nodded.

Here's a new pair of gloves, he said. *I'll show you how to clean everything and pack it up.*

As I put on the gloves, I noticed my hands were shaking. I pulled out the Beretta and the bullet casing and set them down on the table. Cliff came over with the white cloth and the small bottle of clear liquid. As he poured some of the liquid onto the cloth, he said, *Go ahead and unload your weapon.*

I tried to screw off the noise suppressor, but my hands were shaking so badly all I could do was grip the gun tightly in my fists.

Cliff looked at me. Then he reached over and put a gloved hand on mine to stop the shaking.

Why don't you watch me do this one? You'll get plenty of practice.

He slowly took the gun from my hands. I watched him methodically unload the gun, and then clean it, the noise suppressor, the bullets, and the used casing. He wrapped everything up in bubble wrap, taped it up, and put it all in a large pre-addressed packing envelope, and then sealed the envelope. He took off his gloves and reached out a hand for mine. I yanked them off and handed them over, my hands still jumping around like crazy.

You go lie down now, OK? Cliff said. *You've got adrenaline coursing through your body. You just gotta let it pass. I'll book us a flight out of here tomorrow morning.*

I nodded and went to my room. I lay down in the bed.

Control your thoughts, I told myself. I closed my eyes and I saw Fred Hitchens' face, his eyes widening as he saw me.

Control your thoughts.

I heard the sound of the bullet echoing in the garage.

Control your thoughts.

I saw Fred Hitchens shrug at the gods in exasperation.

When I was a child, sometimes other kids' parents would take us to the wave pool. Later that night, when I lay down to sleep, I would feel like my body was back on the waves, floating up and down as each wave rose and fell, rose and fell.

I closed my eyes. I let go.

I let the blood and bullets course through me. Rise and fall, rise and fall.

I felt the heat of it enter my body. I was alive with it. I was untouchable.

· · · ·

I was woken by the sound of my phone ringing. I was lying fully clothed in bed. The clock on the nightstand said it was 10:12pm.

Hello? I mumbled.

It's Charlie.

Charlie?

I talked to Cliff. Good job, kid. Gold star.

He hung up. I put down my phone, then fell back onto the pillow. I exhaled. The waves had finally crested. Now I lay in the shallows, feeling calmer than I ever had.

· · · ·

Cliff and I took an early morning flight back to LAX. As we waited for the plane to board, he asked me questions and I told him every detail I could remember about the killing, including how I felt afterward.

As we sat on the plane, me drinking a celebratory beer, him drinking a seltzer water, Cliff said, *Maybe you've got something there, letting yourself ride out your feelings.*

You think? I said.

I'll tell you the truth, I wasn't sure you could handle this job, Cliff said.

Yeah, I said, quietly.

You ask too many questions. You wonder too much about too many things. You're too damn interested in it all.

I know, I said.

But then you got in there and you did it. You didn't panic. You just acted. Do you know how rare that is for a first time? So maybe it's different for you. Maybe your mind wanders. Maybe that's not such a problem.

Really? I said.

Cliff frowned. *But there may be other things you've got to careful of*, he said.

Like what? I said.

Certain behaviors to look out for. Maybe there won't be any. Or maybe you find you start dragging out the stakeout because you like watching them. Maybe you're tempted to confront the mark just to have some interaction with them. Maybe you start taking liberties with the kills. I don't know. But find out what your weaknesses are, whatever gets you doing things that make you feel sick inside, and steer clear of them.

Then I can just let my mind do what it wants? I asked.

I didn't say that. I'm saying your mind is like a feral fucking cat, and I doubt anyone can control it. But your actions, you can control. Keep them nice and efficient like yesterday, and you're gonna do just fine.

• • • •

After the taxi dropped me off at my motel, I got into the Ford Fusion and drove out toward the hills. Along the way, I stopped at a liquor store to buy a pack of cigarettes.

Years earlier, I had quit what my Husband had called A Disgusting Habit, but I had made a decision during the return trip to LA. At the liquor store, I looked at the rows of cigarettes behind the checkout and, on impulse, asked for a pack of cloves, the kind I used to smoke when I was a teenager.

I parked my car high above the city, then walked off the road, into the dirt and sagebrush. I looked out at the lights of the city spread around me. I tapped out my pack of cigarettes, then put one to my lips and lit it. The smell of cloves made me think of summer nights, sitting on rooftops, cheap beer, careless boys.

On the way back to my motel, I stopped at the same liquor store and bought a bottle of whiskey and two packs of Marlboro's. On the way out, I threw the pack of cloves into the trash.

I had been flirting with nostalgia. There was no wisdom in that.

I was a killer of men.

• • • •

Charlie took me out to celebrate. He had said I could choose the restaurant, so I had him meet me at the 50's diner in the mall in Culver City. I ordered a caramel pecan sundae and Charlie got a root beer.

I have something for you, he said after we sat down. He handed me a square flattish box. *Open it discreetly*, he said.

I carefully lifted the edge of the lid and peered inside. It was a gun—a Glock 17.

Is it mine? I said in a hushed voice. It looked exactly like the gun I'd used to shoot Bud Lander.

One just like it. Only this one doesn't have deaths on it.

Thank you, I said.

You'll probably never have to use a weapon while you're in town, but you still wanna have the option. Especially when you're staying in a motel as awful as yours.

I looked up at Charlie. He winked. I hadn't told him about the motel, but Charlie always seemed to know everything.

The waitress came by with our orders. Charlie clinked his root beer glass against my sundae glass.

To your success, he said.

• • • •

For the next job, and every job after that, Cliff would call me on The Charlie Phone and tell me which city to fly into on which day, and I would book a flight, a rental car, and a hotel. Once I got into town, I would pick up the car, as well as my weapon and the dossier, and then I would check into the hotel.

And then the stakeout would begin. It always involved sitting in a car for hours, covertly following the mark in my vehicle and sometimes on foot. It involved trying to look unobtrusive and casual in any situation—whether pursuing a mark down a dark street at night, or purchasing groceries at the checkout one lane away from them.

Sometimes the dossier included a lot of information about the mark—detailed notes about their schedule, including when they would be by themselves and unguarded. Sometimes there would be information about their security systems or which windows in their houses were left unlocked. Sometimes none of that information would be included, and I'd have to watch the mark closely to learn their habits.

But my stakeouts rarely lasted more than a few days. It turned out that it didn't take much time to get a sense of who a person was and when they'd be most vulnerable. It was never long before I'd start forming a plan.

Following Cliff's advice from the first job, I tried to always enter into a situation I'd already observed—a mark leaving the office, or arriving home at the end of the day, or stepping outside for his last cigarette of the night, that kind of thing. I planned for what I thought would happen and I planned for every eventuality I could. I always had a reason constructed in my mind for why I was at a given place at a given time.

And then there was the killing. This required different skills. If I had planned well—and I planned well—then I had honed in on a perfect moment to step into a person's life and quickly end it, just as Cliff had told me to do. The trick was to not hesitate, but to act at the exact second the moment arose—enter the scene, take aim, and pull the trigger. Make it so it's over before the mark even knows I'm there.

There was something else to acting quickly, I suspected. I thought that if I really stopped to consider what I was doing—squeezing a piece of metal to force another piece of metal into the body of another person, thereby ending that person's life and resulting in the number in my bank account getting bigger—then I never could have done it. It would have seemed laughably ridiculous. The trick of the killing was to do all my thinking beforehand, so once I was in the moment, all I had to do was act. That didn't mean the moment was calm. In the seconds it took to complete, I was always almost overwhelmed by the sensations of panic in my body and the deafening sound of my pounding heart. But I relied on my instincts, and acted before my brain could fully catch up.

After it was done, I would return to my hotel room and lie still. The memories of the killing would course through me, hot rushing waves.

And then, once the fever had passed, I would feel a rare and steady calm. Every time.

I killed a man in Houston as he was unlocking his front door. I killed a man in Seattle while he was walking his dog. I killed a man in the parking lot outside a bowling alley in Topeka. I killed a man while he was repainting the fence in his backyard. I only killed one woman, and I killed her just after she'd let me into her foyer. I killed each of them with a gunshot to the forehead or the back of the skull, except for the woman, who turned her head as I pulled out my gun. I shot her in the cheek and *then* the forehead.

Occasionally, things didn't go according to plan. The second time I entered a mark's home, I was waiting behind the front door and the mark unexpectedly entered through the back door. He saw me and took off running, and I had to shoot him in the back, several times, as he ran across his backyard.

Once, a nervous-looking guy made me when I was following him during the stakeout—he suddenly revved his engine and sped away from me. I didn't bother trying to catch up. I got a new rental car the following day and watched his house for another three days before he appeared again, and then I gunned him down.

Another time, I was in the backseat of the mark's unlocked car, waiting for him to come out of the bar and get into his car so I could shoot him. I watched as the mark approached his car—and then saw he had a buddy with him. I overcame my instinct to run, and instead holstered my gun and lay down on the backseat. When the mark opened his car door, I yelled in my best approximation of a drunken voice, *Get out of my car! I'm trying to sleep!* The two men chuckled and coaxed the seemingly drunk woman out of the car. I had to wait until the next day to kill the mark in his home.

But I never screwed up badly—I was never caught in the act by another person, I never got into a physical altercation with a mark, and I never let my guard down. And in spite of what Charlie had warned me, there wasn't much that was gory about it. A bullet hole in the head, sometimes the smell of shit. I didn't look too closely.

Between jobs, I returned to my shitty motel in LA. After the first few hits, Cliff would come by and I would tell him, in detail, how the job had gone. He was pleased with my progress, I could tell, and he told me Charlie was pleased too.

You still don't hesitate, Cliff said to me once. We were sitting around the little table in my room. *I've never seen anything like it.*

It seemed like a compliment, but he was giving me a strange look.

What? I said.

It's just, I've worked with a lot of people. And most of them have to be taught that. To act before the doubts and questions can creep in. But you just act. I saw it that first time—when you shot Bud Lander outside that bar. The moment he came at you, you fired your weapon. I told Charlie you had to be a professional, but he didn't think so. He said you were a natural.

Cliff was still frowning.

What do you think? I asked.

Well, I don't think he's wrong. But this is how I'd put it. I think you have a killing instinct like none I've ever seen. And I think Charlie thinks he's found himself a perfect little machine. But people aren't machines, Fidge. And if something sets you on the wrong track, I'm worried what that instinct could do. I'm worried you could hurt someone you're not supposed to. Or hurt yourself.

I swallowed. My whole life I was worried about that too. But I'd thought this job would give me some kind of boundaries, boundaries that would hold me in and keep me safe. But now Cliff didn't seem to think so.

It's going fine so far, though. I said. *I feel calm. I feel in control.*

That's good. No strange behaviors cropping up?

No, I said.

OK then. Keep doing what you're doing, Cliff said. *I won't be coming by any more—Charlie doesn't think you need it. But be careful. If you feel like something in you is coming undone, you take yourself out of that situation. No matter what. Got it?*

Got it, I said. It was only later, long after Cliff left, that I realized I didn't know what *coming undone* meant, or how it was any different from how I normally felt.

• • • •

Months into the work, I had a job in New York City for the first time. After I picked up my weapon and the rental car, I sat in my hotel room and read the dossier.

The mark's name was Gian Marino, 51 years old. He owned several Italian restaurants in New York City and had a wife and three children. There was a home address—a condo in Lincoln Square—as well as the directive to not take him out in his home.

In the early morning, I drove to Lincoln Square and found a parking space on the street, across from the entrance to his building. The building was a tall glass structure with neatly manicured potted plants on either side of the entrance, and doormen in white dress shirts with black vests.

I watched many people come out of the building—mostly slim women in yoga pants and men with briefcases, as well as some small children, accompanied by what I guessed were nannies.

Just after 8am, Gian Marino came out in exercise clothes. He was attractive, in a typical kind of way—he had a lot of dark hair, a nice face, a toned physique. I watched him disappear, jogging, down the block, then waited until he returned, flushed and sweating, about 45 minutes later, and went back into his building. An hour later, he reappeared again, this time in a suit. He looked better in a suit.

One of the doormen hailed him a cab. I followed.

I followed Gian Marino all day—from one of his restaurants in SoHo to another in Hell's Kitchen, to a lunch meeting with another man, back to his condo, and then back to the first restaurant, where he remained for several hours.

As I often did, I found myself wondering who had arranged the hit. On one hand, the directive to not take Gian Marino out at home would suggest it was the wife who had arranged it. On the other hand, the dossier hadn't included a very complete schedule, which suggested it was someone who didn't know his comings and goings that well.

He likely had many business associates—was it someone who wanted to take his place? Someone he'd pissed off? Or perhaps it *was* personal—maybe it was his wife's lover and he didn't want to risk her getting harmed or traumatized by the hit.

A little after midnight, Gian Marino emerged from his restaurant and headed north on foot. I got out of the car and followed him. As we were walking down the next block, he abruptly turned his head and looked behind him. I made brief eye contact, abiding by Cliff's advice: *don't pretend you're invisible.* His gaze slid over me, and then he turned back and kept walking.

That was interesting—Gian Marino was afraid of being seen. Was he doing something he shouldn't?

I slowed my pace a little to let more distance open between us.

After a few blocks, he walked up to a brick apartment building. He pressed the buzzer, said something in a low voice, and was let in.

I stopped in front of the building, ostensibly to fish something out of my shoulder bag. I glanced at the buzzer. He had rung the bell for Donna Mathews.

I kept walking, then circled around the block. I took a chance and returned to my car, then drove to Donna Mathews' apartment. I knew I had risked losing him, but after an hour or so, Gian Marino emerged from the building, straightening his tie. Donna Mathews' apartment didn't have a doorman, so he hailed his own cab. I followed the cab until it dropped him off, then watched him re-enter his building for, I assumed, the rest of the night.

The next morning, I was back outside Gian Marino's building at 7:30am. Once again, he came out in jogging clothes just after 8:00am. This time I followed him, slowly, in the car, to see where his run took him.

The rest of the day was similar to the day before—he stopped in at several of his restaurants, attended meetings, and then returned to one of his restaurants for the dinner service. It was Saturday and he remained inside later, then emerged with a group of his staff around 1:30am.

I followed them as they headed to a nearby bar, then waited outside in my car. Before long, Gian Marino emerged with a leggy brunette who worked at his restaurant. They didn't touch or even really look at each other as they climbed into a cab. But as I followed them, I saw them embrace in the backseat of the taxi. Donna Mathews, perhaps?

But the taxi took them to a different apartment building in the area. I watched them disappear inside. Perhaps, I thought, it was the wife who had ordered the hit after all. Gian Marino was inside for maybe two hours this time, then came out and took a cab home.

On Sunday, he went for his morning run and then didn't reemerge from his apartment building again. Maybe he was spending the day with his family? I sat and waited, but by 10:00pm, he still hadn't emerged, and I returned to my hotel. I needed to make a plan.

It wasn't easy to take someone out in New York City, particularly Manhattan. There were people everywhere, especially during the day, and at night, Gian Marino was rarely alone.

Well, I knew one of his weaknesses. What if I tried to seduce him? I would have to have myself arranged as the kind of woman he would be interested in. I'd have to get a decent haircut, and I'd have to shave my legs. I would have to get my makeup done at a department store or something and I'd have to get a tight little dress and high heels.

And then maybe I'd sit at the bar at one of his restaurants. Give him a glance that let him know I liked the look of him. Let him take me back to a hotel room I'd rented just for the occasion. Let him peel the dress off me, push me to the bed, spread my thighs and fuck me. Let him come inside of me.

Of course, it was a terrible idea. It would take a great deal of effort and time to get me to even resemble the kind of woman Gian Marino would want to fuck. And picking him up at one of his restaurants and taking him to a hotel would defeat the efforts Charlie had me take to be untraceable. Finally, the fact that I never had any contact with the mark gave me some kind of protection, I felt, from getting into the Bad Place that Charlie had mentioned.

Still, I was surprised—and a little discomfited—by how much the idea appealed to me. The mark not only seeing me, but *wanting* me. His come still trickling down my leg as I put a bullet in his head.

• • • •

On Monday morning, I returned to Lincoln Square. I waited under an overpass near Gian Marino's building. When he came jogging by, I let him pass, and then shot him in the back of the head. He fell instantly.

• • • •

In between jobs, I did what I called *training*. I didn't see Cliff or Jay or The Locksmith anymore, but I figured I could train myself. I went to the gym every day, sometimes twice a day. I drove all over the city, mastering tight turns and quick exits. I went to the shooting range and then, when I got bored of that, drove out to abandoned lots and shot cans or pieces of trash or, sometimes, small birds, though I always felt bad about that afterwards.

I avoided the bars. When I wanted something to drink, I'd pick up a bottle from the liquor store and bring it back to my motel room.

Now that I was several months into it, the post-kill calm didn't last as long as it had in the beginning. A few days after the killing, I began to feel a kind of itching impatience. Sometimes I felt like within me there was a lit fuse, and I was always relieved when the phone rang and I picked it up to hear Cliff's voice, telling me about the next job. It was the only thing that could douse the fuse.

• • • •

I was in Boise, Idaho, parked outside the home of a mark whose name was also Mark—Mark Harris. He was a 42-year-old white male with no children. He lived in a nice middle-class neighborhood with his partner, Carl Holmgren, who was 39. The dossier included extensive details about Mark Harris and his schedule, so even though this was only my third day following him, I was preparing to make the hit. I had the information I needed, and besides, waiting around in an unknown car would start to attract attention in a quiet neighborhood like the one Mark Harris lived in.

It was 4:45pm. Mark Harris would arrive home from work at about 5:30pm. It was time to go in.

The house was a neat suburban home, built in the 1950's. I walked casually across the front yard to the side gate, slipped on a pair of gloves, and let myself into the backyard.

As was outlined in the dossier, there was a garden shed in the backyard. When I opened it, I found the ladder. I carried the ladder out of the shed, leaned it up under the bathroom window, climbed it, and popped off the window screen. The window was unlocked, as promised. I slipped inside.

The house felt still and silent, unoccupied. It was clear that the job had been arranged either by Mark Harris' partner or by someone else who was close enough to him to know his home and habits. I put the window screen back on and returned to the backyard to replace the ladder.

Back inside, I looked for a good place to wait. It was ideal to find a spot where, once the mark had come inside and closed the door, I could easily step into a good position to shoot him. I could always choose a hidden spot like a closet, but I didn't like to be concealed. It made me feel more vulnerable, and besides, hiding in a closet got boring fast.

I decided to sit at the small table in the kitchen. There was a wall concealing the kitchen from the entryway, and I could hide behind the wall when I heard the mark enter, then turn the corner, aim, and shoot.

It was 4:55pm. I still had a half hour or so. Even though it comprised so much of my job, I hated waiting. I took out my gun and screwed on the suppressor. It was a Sig Sauer P210, one of my favorite weapons. I wondered where the guns Charlie sent me came from, and where they went after I returned them. Did I ever get the same weapon back, or were they only ever used once? Did they arrive to me clean, only to be automatically made dirty by my use, forever stained—figuratively speaking—with blood?

I walked over to the refrigerator. There were a few photos stuck to the fridge with magnets. A wedding announcement, and a couple school photos of children that I assumed were nieces and nephews, or belonged to friends—this definitely wasn't a house with little kids.

There was a photo of Mark Harris with his arm around another man I knew to be Carl Holmgren. At this point in the stakeout, I always felt like I knew the mark a little bit, and seeing him in the photo was like recognizing a friend. He was a tall and gangly man, with long limbs and a dusting of freckles across his cheeks. He had a way of angling his face away from people when they spoke to him that reminded me of a teenager. But he had a startlingly radiant smile that opened up his face like a light turning on. He was smiling like that in the photo, his cheek pressed against Carl Holmgren's.

How often did a current partner order the hit? For all my guessing, I never found out.

I opened the fridge. It was clean, and organized neatly. There was an opened bottle of white wine and an unopened bottle of sparkling wine. There was a bottle of fancy fresh-squeezed orange juice and a plastic container of cut fruit. I could see that the crisper drawers were full of fresh produce. There was a jar of pesto, sausages wrapped in butcher paper, and an expensive cut of salmon. There was a glass reusable container with a green plastic lid, and a post-it note stuck to the lid that read *Eat Me!* with a little smiley face. I took out the container and pried open the lid. Inside was a piece of spinach lasagna. It looked good.

I put the lid back on, and peeled off the post-it note. I wondered if Carl had written the note for Mark, or the other way around. If they were leaving little notes like this for each other, why had Carl arranged to have Mark killed? I crumbled the note in my gloved hand and let it fall to the floor.

Suddenly, I heard the front door opening. I closed the refrigerator door and flattened myself against the wall shielding me from the entryway. My heart was pounding hard. An ocean started to roar in my ears. I slowly pulled out my weapon.

I heard the jingle of keys, and the sound of the door closing. I heard the slide of shoes being removed and a soft sigh. It was obviously just one person. I quickly peered around the wall. I saw Mark Harris, looking down at the mail in his hands. I took a breath and whipped around the corner, gun out. Mark Harris lifted his head as I aimed my weapon. I pulled the trigger. It didn't move.

We both stared at each other, in shock. I glanced down at the gun, and realized the safety was still on.

Mark Harris threw his arms up, and the mail in his hands went showering down around him. He scrambled away from me, until his back hit the wall. He was shouting, *Please! Please!*

My gun was still aimed at his head. *Into the living room*, I commanded, in a Movie Bad Guy kind of voice.

He looked at the door, and I could tell he was thinking of running. *Flight*, Cliff would have said.

Now! I yelled.

Shrinking a little, Mark Harris stepped into the living room, his arms still raised.

On your knees, I said.

He sank down to the carpet, then looked up at me. His eyes were the color of the sea. He was crying. He said, *Why are you doing this?*

Look at the floor, I said sharply.

He crouched to the floor, his hands clutching at the rug. *Why are you doing this?* he cried into the carpet.

I lifted my thumb and slid the safety off.

Why are you doing this? he said again, like a chant he thought could save him. *Why are you doing this? Why are you doing this?*

I pulled the trigger. The bullet hit him in the top of the head. His body lurched forward, then crumbled to the floor.

I reached down and grabbed his shoulder, then gently pushed him onto his back. His eyes were closed. There was blood running down his face. Sometimes you can look at flesh and just know it's dead.

I reached down and ran my gloved finger through the blood on his cheek, then put my finger in my mouth. I'd always liked the taste of blood.

I pulled my finger out of mouth and stared at it. I had sucked it clean. What the fuck was I doing?

After I left Mark Harris' house, I drove for several miles until I reached a Walmart, and pulled into the parking lot. I got out of the car and vomited onto the pavement.

I spat a few times, then climbed back into the car. Why hadn't I shot him before he could say anything? And, even before that, how had I forgotten to take the safety off my gun? My relationship to my weapon was so intimate, I ought to be able to operate it without thinking.

Maybe I had been too cocky. Or maybe I was getting sloppy.

Or maybe, a voice said, *something you saw in that house upset you.*

Things had gone wrong on the job before, but I'd never felt like this. Like some kind of tremor was moving through me.

Why are you doing this? Why are you doing this? chanted in my mind like a song I'd gotten stuck in my head.

. . . .

I drove straight to a bar. I took a seat and ordered a whiskey. I tossed it back. I ordered another. I stared straight ahead of me. The bar wasn't full but there were enough people—men—in there. I didn't look around or try to find one who looked good to me.

I didn't have to wait long. I felt the form of a large man sit next to me.

Hey there, he said. It wasn't a very friendly sounding voice.

Hey, I said.

You looking for a date?

I looked over at him. Beard, blank eyes.

Sure, I said.

What'll it cost me for the full deal?

Ah. An exchange of labor for money. This I could understand, though I had no idea what the going rate was.

Fifty, I said, *but no kissing or blow jobs.*

Deal, he said. *My truck's parked outside.*

I finished my drink and followed him out. He drove a four-door Dodge Ram truck that was about fifteen years old, but looked to be in good condition. I started to climb into the backseat.

Hey, he hissed. *Not here. Get in the front.*

I looked blankly at him, then got into the front seat.

He shook his head, then got into the driver's seat.

He started the car. *I know a spot where no one'll bother us*, he said.

He pulled out of the parking lot. It was just getting dark. Was he going to try to kill me? I squeezed my arm against my side so I could feel my gun press into my ribcage. If he had a gun on him, he might beat me to the draw. He probably would not.

We drove for almost ten minutes, down one empty road after another, until we reached a big, deserted-looking warehouse. It did seem like a good place to kill someone. But then, it also seemed like a good place to bring a hooker. He pulled into the gravel parking lot, then turned off his truck.

He reached into the back of his jeans. My heart rate jumped and I slid my hand across my stomach, closer to my weapon. He took out his wallet. He counted out fifty dollars, all in fives. He handed it to me in a little bundle. I slipped the money into my jacket pocket, and then I turned and climbed into the backseat of the truck. He followed me.

I unlaced my boots and yanked them off, then pulled off my jeans and underwear in one go. He ran his hand up my thigh.

You've got a pretty little pussy, he said.

It was the only thing he'd said in a friendly kind of way, and I didn't like it. I felt like I might cry.

Come on, then, I said, lying down on the bench seat. He unfastened his belt, unzipped his fly, and got on top of me.

I could tell from the way he moved that he'd taken out his dick. He spat on his hand, then wet it. I'd thought he'd use a condom, but maybe it had been up to me to insist? Too late—he was inside of me.

His dick was reasonably sized, but I had hoped it would be bigger. I had hoped it would be so big I'd feel like he was tearing me apart.

As he fucked me, my head thumped against the car door and I focused on that dull, rhythmic pain.

And then the goddamn song came back.

Why are you doing this? Why are you doing this?

Thump, thump, thump.

Why are you doing this? Why are you doing this?

Thump, thump, thump.

Why are you doing this? Why are you doing this?

Why are you doing this? Why are you doing this? Why are you doing this? Why are you doing this? Why are you doing this? Why are you doing this? Why are you doing this? Why are you doing this? Why are you doing this? Why are you doing this? Why are you doing this? Why are you doing this? Why are you doing this? Why are you doing this? Why are you doing this? Why are you doing this?

Harder, I said, *fuck me harder.*

He kept going.

I closed my eyes and gripped the shoulder of his jacket. I wanted to disappear.

He finished with a groan and collapsed on top of me. I relaxed under the weight of him but within a moment, he was up again, and climbing back to the front seat.

I pulled on my underwear and pants, then my boots. I wiped off my face, which was wet. I climbed into the passenger's seat.

He was fiddling with his belt buckle.

I could take out my gun right now, I thought. I could shoot him in the temple and blow his brains all over the cabin of this truck.

Then the thought of doing it seemed to shift into maybe something like a plan of doing it. I pulled my arms close and felt the pressure of my gun against my ribs again. It was bigger than his cock.

I gotta go, I said, and reached for the door handle.

Are you crazy? he said. *We're miles from anywhere. Just stay put, I can take you back.*

Breathe through the panic, I reminded myself. I dropped my hand from the door handle. *Ok,* I said, *Take me back.*

• • • •

I had two weeks off between jobs. I spent most of those two weeks in my motel room. *Find out what your weaknesses are and steer clear of them,* Cliff had said. My weaknesses were, perhaps, bars and post-it notes on refrigerated foods. So I stayed in my room and made up home work-out routines. I picked up fast-food once or twice a day, and drank heroic amounts of whiskey, shot by shot.

I was relieved when Cliff called and told me to go to Tucson. I took the flight, I got the rental car, I picked up the dossier, I picked up my weapon, I checked into a hotel. I followed the mark. I wanted to be excited to be in Tucson—I'd always liked the desert—but, even though I was glad I wasn't in my motel room in Los Angeles anymore, I felt a kind of dullness about it

The mark's name was Derek Weins. He was a 47-year-old Black man, married with two children. The dossier noted that on Saturdays, he stayed home while his wife took the children—two pre-teenaged boys—out. On the first Saturday after I arrived, I parked on the street and watched Derek Weins sit on the shaded patio of his little Pueblo-style house. He was reading a newspaper and sipping at a can of Diet Coke. The patio was mostly obstructed from view by some scrubby trees and a couple of cacti.

For some reason, it bothered me how easy it was. It didn't seem fair. But I couldn't get sloppy. Maybe I would walk up to the patio and Derek Weins would be waiting for me with a gun drawn. Then I wondered if it was racist to wonder that.

I put on my gloves, attached the suppressor to my weapon, and stepped out of the car with the gun at my side. I approached the patio. I could see Derek Weins through the trees. His head was bent over his newspaper. I should have aimed my gun, but I didn't. I stepped onto the cement patio and he looked up. He looked surprised, but not alarmed.

Hi there! he said, and smiled. *You looking for someone?*

The perfect moment had come and now it was gone.

I lifted up my gun and pointed it at him. He raised his hands.

Whoa, easy now, he said. *What's this about?*

He seemed concerned, but calm. I wondered if he'd had a gun pointed at him before. Then I wondered if it was racist to wonder *that*.

Look, the house is unlocked, he said. *No one else is here. You go ahead and take whatever you want. I won't get in your way.*

I sat down at the patio table, across from him. He was an attractive man, with large, friendly dark eyes.

I came here to kill you, Derek, I said.

His face changed when I said his name. The situation had become more serious for him. *I see*, he said. *Did someone send you?*

I nodded.

Was it Joe?

Now that was interesting. He already knew who might want him dead. Maybe all the marks did. Maybe I should have been talking to them this whole time. *They never tell me who ordered it*, I said.

So this is just your job, then? Killing people? He glanced into the house, probably thinking of a phone or a weapon he wanted to reach for. I wasn't worried. My gun was pointed directly at his head. I just didn't know why I hadn't shot it yet.

You know, I have access to a lot of money, he said. *Whatever they're paying you, I can double it.*

It's not just about the money, I said. *The job is...it's kind of a calling.*

I don't know who you are or what this is, but trust me, sweetheart, what you're doing is not a calling, he said.

I suddenly had the feeling I had lost the upper hand. This was why you didn't get into a conversation with the mark.

Maybe not, I said. *But I've done this many times. And I haven't screwed it up yet. Is there anything you want to say before you die?*

He looked at me, and his face kind of sagged. *What would I say? You're just doing your job, so nothing I could say would make any difference, would it?*

Not to whether you live or die, no, I said.

And you're not exactly going to pass on my dying words to my wife and kids, are you?

No, I said.

So who would my words be for, then? You? What could I possibly say that would make any sense to you?

I shrugged. He was right, of course. So why did I suddenly feel so shitty?

Will you do me a favor? he said. *Will you call the police after you do it? My wife and kids are coming home, and I don't want them to be the ones to, you know, to find my...my body.* Tears started falling down his face.

OK, I said.

You promise me?

I promise, I said. He seemed to relax just a little. Then I shot him in the head. He toppled back in his chair, then fell to the ground.

I peered over. The force of the bullet had blown off part of his skull—there was a wild splatter of blood and brains on the patio floor.

I sat there for a moment. Charlie would not be pleased that I had drawn this out. But then, I realized, he wouldn't actually know. The only ones who knew what had happened were me and the mark. In fact, I could say whatever I wanted to say to the mark before I killed him. After all, conversation left no imprint. The promise I had made to Derek Weins, which of course I wouldn't keep, had already vanished, except from my memory. And from the memory of Derek Weins, before I killed him. I looked over at the mess of brains on the patio. Was that promise recorded there somewhere?

I suddenly felt a strong urge to cradle a piece of those brains in my hands.

I remembered Charlie's warning about insides on the outside. I stood up. I had to leave now.

I found the bullet casing and pocketed it and then started to walk back toward my car, but something stopped me. I looked back at the body. Maybe leaving so soon after the killing was what was bringing me down. Maybe I was robbing myself of having a complete experience. I returned to the body and knelt down beside it.

The pieces of brain were all different sizes. I had thought they'd be gray up close but they were a kind of pinkish red. I reached out and picked up a piece with my hand. It was soft and wet and lighter than I'd expected. It had some spring to it when I squeezed it with my fingers. I tossed it down and picked up another small piece. This one had some hard eggshell-like pieces stuck to it that I realized were skull fragments. I set it down. I looked at the head and the big hole that was still full of brains. I took a breath and stuck my hands inside.

I woke up in a kind of panic. I was lying in my hotel bed in Tucson, my head throbbing from the whiskey I'd drunk the night before.

I didn't feel that I had made good choices. And now the killing was over but I didn't feel calm at all. I felt like I'd ruined something, somehow.

I reminded myself that no one knew what I'd done. No one knew about the conversation I'd had with Derek Weins, or how I'd handled his brains afterwards. No one would ever know. Which was almost like it never happened.

I took a long pull from the bottle of whiskey I'd left lying on the bed, took a hot shower, then threw on some clothes and stumbled down to the buffet breakfast.

The colors of the hotel—like most places in Tucson—were all muted desert tones. Terracotta, sage, sand. It was hot outside but the breakfast room was shudderingly cold from the air-conditioning. I suddenly felt that I hated Tucson.

I made my way through the buffet, filling my plate, then took a seat next to a window that looked out on a little cactus garden. I picked up my fork and surveyed my breakfast. Scrambled eggs, bacon, a couple shriveled sausage links, toasted white bread, and a pale slice of cantaloupe. I put down the fork, then reached my hand into the scrambled eggs. They were not exactly like brains, but they were *enough* like brains. I dropped the eggs, and wiped my hand off on the paper napkin. Then I stood, and left the table. It was time to get back to LA.

. . . .

Even though the flight to LA was short, I felt revived once I landed at the airport. I stopped in a diner on the way home and got a very large, very cold chocolate milkshake.

Back at my hotel, I took a cleansing shot of whiskey and showered. I put on clean clothes. I was barely shaking anymore. Charlie would have no idea I'd gone off the rails, just a little. All I had to do was get back to how I'd been at the beginning of the work. In quick, out quick.

There might have been a certain remove to doing the job quickly, and there might have been something in that remove that made me feel like I could fall apart in despair, but I just had to recognize that maintaining a distance from my work was better than the alternative. If I let the job take me in all the directions it could, if I wandered down the different paths offered by a final conversation or a torn apart body, I risked losing my way and never being able to find the path again.

· · · ·

I was in Acworth, Georgia, waiting outside yet another house. Parts of Georgia were atmospheric—swampy and ancient and haunted, but the neighborhood I was in had nondescript houses and wide, boring lawns. I could have been anywhere, on any number of jobs I'd already done. And then the mark stepped out the front door and my heart dropped.

He looked exactly like my former boyfriend, Doug. I watched him walk down the long driveway to the mailbox. He was tall, with a loping stride—long arms and long legs. He had a slight beard and the same kind of lumberjack clothes Doug used to wear—Carhartt's and flannel, work boots. The same smooth forehead, the same easy expression.

It wasn't Doug, of course. The mark's name was Jason Rainger and I could see, as he got closer, that his face was made of broader planes and he wasn't, I didn't think, as tall as Doug.

I watched him get his mail and re-enter his house. Jason Rainger worked from home doing some kind of computer job, and he lived alone. Aside from the long walk up his driveway during which I'd be exposed, it would be easy enough to enter his house and take him out. But I'd watch him first.

I waited outside the house for hours. When Jason Rainger finally came out again, I felt that same shock of recognition, even though I knew it wasn't Doug. I followed him to the hardware store, then back home. He didn't appear again, and once it was past midnight, I returned to my hotel.

I sat on my hotel room bed. Doug and I had started dating when I was twenty and he was twenty-one—more than ten years ago. We were together for just over a year. We weren't much alike. I heard more than one person describe him as a *big kid*, and that had always stuck with me. He laughed a lot and got excited by everything and would lift me off the ground in his big arms. He grew up in the woods with, like, six brothers and he called each one of them every Sunday. We broke up after I cheated on him. Well, after I told him about how many times I had cheated on him. But when we were still together, Doug made me feel like there was nothing in the world that I had to be ashamed of.

His name was Doug Aldi. I searched and found what I thought was him on Facebook, though the thumbnail was so small it was hard to tell. He lived in Pittsburgh. I hesitated before clicking on his page, afraid that this was the type of behavior I was trying to avoid, and then reminded myself that it had nothing to do with work. I was merely looking up an ex-boyfriend. It was, in fact, was one of the most normal things a person could do. I clicked on the link.

The photo on his page was much larger. It was definitely Doug. He was so much more Doug than the not-Doug I'd been following. His eyes were blue and his smile was wide, with that one slightly crooked front tooth.

I kept looking through his page. I saw a photo of him with his arms around two small children. Maybe they're his nephews, I thought. And I saw several photos of a thin blonde woman, clearly his girlfriend. But they might have broken up by now.

After hours of scrolling, I finally reached Doug's very first post. I had looked at every photo and every post on his page. It was nearly four in the morning. He was definitely married, and those were definitely his children. They both had very blond hair and looked like television commercial children. Doug looked happy. Well, it would be easy to be happy when you were as simple-minded as Doug, I thought. I went to bed.

· · · ·

I watched Not-Doug for five days. I followed him to the grocery store, back to the hardware store, to the bar, and to a friend's house, where they drank beer and smoked cigarettes on the porch. I was aware of the doubling I was doing—I saw Doug and I also saw Jason Rainger. Jason Rainger, whose life seemed so dull and pointless. Why did anyone want to kill Jason Rainger? Why did anyone want to kill anyone, when our lives were all so ineffectual?

And why was it that Doug, with his boring life and his boring Facebook page, was occupying so many of my thoughts? It unnerved me.

But now I had the opportunity to kill his doppelganger. Not just the opportunity, in fact, I was *supposed* to do it—it was my *job* to kill him.

Maybe this job was just what I needed to get back on track. Maybe killing not-Doug could finally make things clear and easy again, like they had been at the beginning. Maybe it would be a kind of rebirth.

· · · ·

I followed not-Doug for a few more days, although I knew I was dragging it out for too long. I watched him get in a fight outside a bar that was quickly broken up. I watched him take his car through a car wash. I stopped trying to figure out who would want him dead. The fact of Jason Rainger as an actual person was becoming a little hazy to me.

On Sunday evening, I watched not-Doug walk into his usual bar, and I resolved to kill him the following morning. Most people in his neighborhood would be at work, and not-Doug would likely be at least a little hungover. I returned to my hotel for the night.

I arrived at his house early in the morning. I watched him walk down to the mailbox. He was wearing blue jeans, a red flannel, and slippers. I didn't think I'd ever seen the real Doug wear slippers.

I sat in my rental car for a few minutes and then I walked up the driveway. It would have been better to wait until not-Doug left, then wait inside his house for him to return, as I usually did when I entered a mark's home, but I wasn't worried. I felt killing him would be very easy.

The door was unlocked. I let myself in. The house felt small and close. It had ugly old carpeting and a couple of cheap posters on the walls.

I walked through the living room to a hallway. I turned the corner and saw him in the room at the end of the hall. His back was to me—he was sitting on a chair, facing his computer.

I could have shot him, but I did not. I knew I wasn't going to rush this. I did not think my vow to be in quick and out quick applied to this situation. This was, after all, my Rebirth.

I walked all the way up to him and pressed the tip of my gun against his skull. I was about to tell him not to move but he started wildly and turned around, then scrambled out of his chair. He was making a big fuss, and yelling things like, *Who are you? What do you want? Don't shoot me!*

It wasn't Doug's voice.

Shut up, I said, in my Movie Bad Guy voice. He stopped yelling. He looked scared.

Stand up, I said.

He was kind of crouched against the desk but, with great effort, he stood up straight.

Take off those slippers, I said.

Wh—what? He stuttered. He was staring at my gun.

I said take off those slippers! I yelled in the Bad Guy voice. He kicked them off.

I looked at him. Something was off. Up close, he didn't look like Doug at all.

Take off your shirt, I said softly.

This time, he didn't ask any questions. He unbuttoned his flannel. He wasn't wearing anything underneath it. The hair on his chest was light, and he had a little rounded belly. I couldn't remember what Doug's chest had looked like, but I felt a little relieved by the sight. He didn't *not* look like Doug, anyway.

Now take off your pants, I said.

Wh—why? he said. *What do you want? I didn't do anything! Please!*

I pointed the gun at his face. *Take off your pants,* I said again.

His mouth gaped open in a kind of frozen expression of fear. He unzipped his jeans and took them off. He was wearing blue plaid boxer shorts. His legs were very long.

I took a step toward him and placed my hand against his chest. His skin was warm under my palm. His breath came in jagged gasps. I stepped closer to him and pressed the side of my face to his chest.

Put your arms around me, I said.

I was worried he'd stutter more questions, but he'd gone quiet. He put his arms around my shoulders, gingerly. I felt the warmth of his skin through my clothing. He smelled like soap and wood shavings. Something in my chest unhitched.

I realized I was crying. I pulled back and wiped off my face. Then I looked up and saw a strange man staring down at me. He looked confused. I realized with a thrill that he could have easily overpowered me. But it was already too late.

I stepped back, flicked the safety off my gun, and shot him in the head.

He fell against the office chair as he went down, tipping it over on top of him as he landed on the soft carpet. I waited a moment, but he didn't move.

I took a step forward and lifted the chair off his body. His eyes were still open, blue and blank, and his blood was darkening the carpet beneath him.

I had confirmed he was dead. Now would be the time to leave. Instead, I set the chair down on the carpet and took a seat. I looked at not-Doug. His face looked dead, of course, but the rest of his body seemed so innocently alive. The small pink nipples, the darkening hair that ran from his belly button to his boxers, the kneecaps, the toes.

How could one make sense of a body?

I needed to think. I wasn't feeling panic or excitement or the calm I'd felt in his arms. I needed to find some other way through this that would still be the right way. I grabbed the pack of Camel's and the lighter off not-Doug's desk. I went back into the hallway, picking up and pocketing the bullet casing as I did. I found the bathroom, which had a built-in bathtub. I climbed inside and sank down, lying in the tub with the top half of my body propped up a little. I lit a cigarette.

I found I could not think. And yet, when I had finished smoking, I realized I'd made a choice. I put the cigarette out in the sink, then put the butt in my back pocket.

I walked through not-Doug's kitchen into his garage. Inside, there were several tables and chairs in the process of being built—it looked like he did some kind of amateur furniture-making in his free time, which explained the trips to the hardware store.

I turned away from the never-to-be-completed chairs, and surveyed his tools. They were very well-organized—everything was either stored in a neatly labeled box, placed in a specific spot on a shelf, or hung against the wall. Seeing that, I felt a kind of respect for not-Doug for the first time.

I found a circular saw and an extension cord, a hacksaw and a jab saw, and a pair of goggles. I brought them all out to the living room, which had more space to move around in than the cramped office. Then I dragged not-Doug's body down the hallway into the living room. As I dragged him, blood from his open head wound left...well, not a trail, exactly, but dark, erratic blood stamps all along the carpet. He stared up blankly.

I moved aside a coffee table and deposited the body in the middle of the living room. I looked at not-Doug and then reached down and, with my gloved fingertips, closed his eyelids. I had been afraid that after I did, the eyelids would snap back open, but they stayed shut.

I took off my leather jacket and laid it on the couch. And then I cut up the body.

It took a long time, and the work was difficult. Even though I tried to only cut at the joints, it was hard getting through some of them, especially the hip bones. I mostly used the hand saws to get through skin and muscle and fat, since they were easier to control, but I had to use the circular saw to remove the legs, which I didn't like because it was noisy and sent blood and bits of bone flying.

It was challenging in other ways I hadn't predicted. Using the hand saws required a lot of effort and my hands started to get sore, followed by my shoulders and neck. The blood and fat made my latex gloves and tools slimy, and they frequently slipped from my hands. In addition, it was harder for me to identify the different organs than I would have thought. I could have looked them up on my phone, but it was tucked into the pocket of my leather jacket, and I didn't want to take it out during the process and get it dirty.

Still, I did my best to take a methodical approach. I cut off the limbs first. Then I cut off the head. Then I cut off the genitals. Then I cut the torso from sternum to, well, just above where the penis had been, and I removed the organs. Blood soaked the carpet. The organs stank. I went to the bathroom to throw up twice.

I laid all the parts very neatly on a patch of clean-ish carpet. Once I was finally done, I surveyed my work.

There were two feet, two lower legs, and two upper legs with knees, though I'd mangled one of the kneecaps. Two upper arms, two lower arms, two hands. There was a penis (circumcised) and a scrotum. Then there was a thoroughly cleaned-out torso. Next to that, there were the organs: the huge unraveling intestines, the kidneys—which were attached to the bladder—a fleshy thing I thought was maybe the pancreas, the liver, the stomach, the spleen, the lungs, and finally, the heart. Next to that was the head, a thudding dull thing now.

Was I better? I wasn't sure. I took off the goggles and went to the bathroom to smoke again. The sight of myself in the mirror was startling. I had blood and...would one call it *gore?*...all over my face, in my hair, and soaking through my clothes. I couldn't exactly leave the house like this.

I lit a cigarette, even though in taking it out, I smeared blood onto the filter. I walked, smoking, to the kitchen, and found a black plastic garbage bag under the sink. Then I went back to the garage and grabbed a pair of work gloves I'd seen earlier.

In the bathroom, I took out my gun and laid it on the bathroom counter, then took the bullet casing out of my pocket and set it next to the gun. Then I removed my boots, my gun holster, my shirt, my bra, my jeans, my underwear and my socks, and put everything except the boots in the black garbage bag. I grabbed the goggles and put them in the bag too. Then I turned on the water and pulled back the shower curtain. I put out my cigarette and tossed the butt into the black plastic bag. Finally, I carefully removed my gloves and threw them into the bag.

I got into the shower, careful not to touch anything. Doug only had a bar of soap and a bottle of shampoo in there. I knocked the bar of soap over with my foot, then lifted it with my toes to my hands. I have always had dexterous feet. I used the soap to get the blood off my body and out of my hair as best I could.

Then I got out of the shower and threw the soap into the black plastic bag. Could they get fingerprints off soap? I didn't know, but I didn't want to risk it.

I put on the work gloves, and relaxed a little. Even though the gloves were way too big, at least my fingers were covered. Treacherous creatures, fingers.

I turned off the shower water and I tied up the black plastic bag. I walked naked into the bedroom and looked through the drawers, until I found a pair of loose black cotton shorts—they looked like sweatpants that had been cut off at the knee—and a green and black flannel shirt. I put the shorts and flannel on, then went back to the bathroom, slipped my feet into my boots, and laced them up. I put the bullet casing in the pocket of the shorts and grabbed my weapon.

In the living room, I put my leather jacket on over the flannel and stuffed my gun into the pocket. I grabbed the plastic bag, looked once more at the pleasingly neat row of parts I had arranged on the carpet, and left the house.

• • • •

I had felt so good when the work was done, but as I drove away from not-Doug's house, I began to feel like a kind of darkness was closing in around me.

I kept trying and failing to get to the center of the thing. I had a strange feeling that I didn't know what it was like to kill a person. I had never killed someone because I wanted to. It was like I had only ever committed half of the deed. Like I came in during the middle of a sex act just to climax. Except I felt no pleasure in it. At the moment, I felt nothing at all.

I drove past strip malls and subdivisions. I found I was crying again. I couldn't bear the thought of returning to my nondescript hotel room. I kept driving.

I drove until the trees around me became more dense, the foliage more lush. I drove into older neighborhoods where all the houses had screened-in porches. Tall oak trees shaded the roads and willow trees dipped their soft branches into the yards. The air seemed thicker here, hot and muggy, and filled with the sounds of buzzing insects. I felt myself relax.

I drove through fancier neighborhoods, with rambling plantation homes and large yards.

I drove into a more urban area, with busier roads, gas stations, and an adult video store.

I drove by a large square-shaped yellow building that had the words THE THIRSTY GATOR hand-painted in huge black letters across the front of it. After I passed, I wondered if it was a bar. I made a U-turn and headed back.

I realized when I stepped inside that it was more of a restaurant than a bar. There was a sandwich sign listing oyster po'boys, alligator bites, and Cajun fries, and several families were seated at tables around the room. There was an actual bar, though, so I sidled up and took a seat.

The bartender made his way over. He was tall and lean and wore a white undershirt that was stained gray around the neck. Above the shirt, the bones of his ribs pressed through his taut, brown chest. His hair was long and he was smoking a cigarette. He grinned with half his mouth.

What can I get you, darling? he said. He ashed his cigarette directly onto the bar floor.

I ordered a whiskey, then pulled out my cigarettes, which were actually not-Doug's Camel's. As I took out a smoke, I noticed there was a streak of blood smeared across the pack, and I tucked it back into my pocket.

I surveyed the room. There were several men sitting by themselves, eating fried food and drinking beer. Most of them were the big burly types I usually went for, who I could pick up as easily as trash on the side of the road. But I found I wanted to fuck the bartender.

I didn't know how exactly to make that happen. I was still wearing not-Brad's oversized flannel and the black shorts, and my hair was damp from the shower. I might have still had blood flecked on parts of my body I hadn't noticed. I had a certain something about me, but it wasn't all that much.

But I liked the bartender's snakey, dirty look. Why couldn't I have what I wanted? As I watched him, he glanced over at me, and I nodded.

Another one? he asked.

Thanks. What's your name? I said.

Troy, he said.

I'm Reese, I said, and felt a secret pleasure using my real name.

Where you from, Reese?

I'm from California, I said.

Well, that makes sense. A beautiful girl from a beautiful place like that.

I smiled, showing my teeth. This might be easier than I thought.

• • • •

I was a little drunk by the time Troy the bartender got off work. He led me to his vehicle, a piece of shit Ford Cargo van. I got inside and saw that the hollowed-out back of the van was filled with junk—a plastic lawn chair, an old TV, fast-food wrappers, beer cans.

Sorry for the mess, he said.

My excitement dimmed a little, though I couldn't tell if that was because of the trash or the apology. I lit a cigarette.

He drove for about fifteen minutes through shaded dark neighborhoods. I kept the window open so that the thick warm air blew through my hair.

We turned onto a long driveway, and drove up toward a startlingly stately colonial-style home. It gleamed white in the moonlight. Troy pulled in front of a wide four-car garage and parked. What the fuck? Was this sleazy bartender some trust fund kid? That did not seem to bode well for the evening.

I stepped out of the van.

This way, he said, and walked toward the garage.

I followed him. He unlocked the door to the garage and stepped inside.

Half of the garage had been converted into a kind of apartment, with a small kitchen, a couple of couches that served as a living area, and a doorway into what I assumed was the bedroom. It was even more of a mess than the car—littered with autoparts and trash.

You want a beer? he asked.

Sure, I said.

As he dug around in the refrigerator, I noticed a dirty paring knife on the kitchen counter. I slipped it into the pocket of my shorts.

He handed me the beer. I opened it and drank half of it down.

Is that the bedroom? I asked.

Sure is, he said. He grinned and took me by the hand.

The room was dark except for the moonlight from outside. A fan blew hot air through the room.

He undressed quickly, excitedly. His body was thin and sinewy, his cock long and hard, the pubic hair plentiful. I slipped out of my clothes and stood naked facing him.

He pulled me to him and kissed me. The night air was warm and the insects thrummed inside my body. I grabbed his cock with my hands, but I felt I had no desire to do anything with it. I let it go. I felt a kind of sinking feeling. He planted a soft wet kiss on my neck.

Hang on, I said. I pulled away and reached for my shorts. I took out the paring knife and held it in front of my face so I could get a good look at it.

What have you got there? he said laughingly.

I slashed the knife across his throat. Blood rivered from his neck. He tried to stop it with his hands, but the blood flowed out between his fingers and down his chest. He stumbled toward me, grabbing at my shoulders, as if I could help him. His body fell against mine, and warm blood spilled onto my face. I opened my mouth. Blood entered my mouth and covered my body. I was finally, finally, *feeling*.

We stumbled to the floor, his body on top of mine. He bled onto me, into me. I surrendered. I was ready to die.

· · · ·

I didn't die, of course. But Troy did. He shuddered on top of me, and then went limp. His body pressed down on me. Slowly, it started to become heavy. The blood was cooling. The thrill was ebbing away.

I pushed his body off of me and stood up.

I was still holding the little paring knife in my fist, but there was nothing left to do.

· · · ·

The next morning, I flew back to LA. I felt worse than I could remember ever having felt. Hungover, but more than that.

Before I'd left Georgia, I had gone to an abandoned homeless encampment under a bridge, where I had made a big fire and burned the clothes I'd worn to the bartender's house, burned the plastic handle of the little paring knife to nothing, burned the contents of the black plastic bag I'd taken from not-Doug's, and burned the dossier on not-Doug. I had also cleaned and returned my firearm, the remaining bullets, and the spent casing. But I still felt like I had left something behind, exposed for the world to see. Like my own organs were splayed out on that carpet.

Once I was back in my motel room in LA, I sat at the little table in my room and smoked—I was back to my own pack, my own brand.

I wanted to get drunk but felt I had to somehow get my mind in order.

From what I could tell, there were three primary causes for concern.

#1: The police. I had behaved stupidly in Georgia. At not-Doug's, I had stayed in the house for much longer than I usually did. I had of course worn gloves the entire time and had collected my cigarette butts, but still. I might have left hairs behind in the bathtub, and I had certainly left my bloody footprints all over the house—footprints from the boots that were currently lying in the corner of my motel room. I'd been even stupider with Troy the bartender. Plenty of people had seen me talking to him at the bar, and I'd even told him my real name. Then after I had killed him, I'd driven his van from his house to The Thirsty Gator to get my rental car, creating the opportunity for more witnesses to see me. I'd no doubt left my DNA all over his vehicle and his home.

#2: Charlie. Charlie would be very disappointed. I felt somehow I had fallen into the darkness he had so patiently tried to save me from. Maybe he always knew I'd succumb to it. That didn't mean he'd forgive it. He might have me killed. Or at least fire me.

#3: The implications regarding my well-being. The killing of not-Doug and the treatment of the body had seemed so right. Red squishy bits all made coherent. And the killing of the bartender had felt *good*. I'd had no reason at all to kill him, and yet it felt more meaningful than any other kill. And whenever I thought about how it felt to be doused in his blood, I wanted to do it again. That couldn't be a good sign.

• • • •

Sometimes I convinced myself that nothing would come of it. Perhaps the police were pursing some imagined local serial killer. Perhaps the two murders would never be connected. Perhaps Charlie figured if Jason Rainger was dead, it didn't matter so much how I'd gone about it. Perhaps I hadn't done anything so bad. Perhaps I was just tired from working too much.

Or perhaps I was a sick fuck and now everyone knew and someone who worked for Charlie was already on their way to come take me out.

• • • •

I thought about how Cliff had once told me that Charlie thought he'd found himself a perfect little machine in me.

I had liked the sound of that. I liked the idea that I could be programmed for a purpose. But then Cliff had said, *But people aren't machines, Fidge.*

Was that why had I done what I did to Jason Rainger and to Troy? Because I wasn't a piece of scientific equipment and wasn't programmable after all?

Or maybe Cliff was wrong. Maybe I was simply malfunctioning. Maybe I was a machine with a heart that was bleeding all over my internal gears, and that was why I had stopped working.

• • • •

I started to imagine my own death. It was the only thing that relaxed me. I hoped it would not be too quick. It occurred to me now that taking someone's life before they even knew what was happening was not a mercy, as I'd always thought. It was a kind of cruelty. They don't even have the chance to reckon with their own death.

But then, I had found out that when you gave a person the chance to reckon with their own death, to at least say some last words, they wasted it with bargaining and tears.

I would not waste my final moments.

I hoped whoever Charlie hired would knock on the door, politely. I would let him in and we'd sit down across the little table from each other. We'd each take a shot of whiskey and I would smoke a last cigarette. Then he would draw his gun—hopefully a black Sig Sauer or maybe a Colt 1911—and I would open my mouth, and rest my lips around the muzzle. His finger would curl over the trigger.

The only pity was I wouldn't be able to watch.

• • • •

I was lying in bed when The Charlie Phone rang. I picked it up and said hello.

That you, kid?

It was Charlie.

Yeah, I said.

Good. You're gonna take a trip to Boston on Tuesday. Find a place in Beacon Hill, it's a real charming neighborhood. Cliff will send you more details about the pick-ups.

My head was spinning. Charlie was calling me about...a job? In spite of what I called it, he had never once called me on The Charlie Phone.

There was silence.

You got that? he said. He sounded a little irritated.

Uh, yeah, I said. *Boston. Tuesday. Beacon Hill.*

Be professional, ok? Not like Acworth.

There was a long pause as Charlie let me figure out exactly what that meant.

Okay, I said quietly. *Not like Acworth.*

Good, he said. Then he hung up.

My hands were shaking as I put them to my face. *Not like Acworth.* That meant Charlie knew about Jason Rainger, and that he didn't know about Troy. It also meant he was going to give me another chance.

I had to get back on track. Do the jobs like I had in the beginning. I could rent a decent apartment and make some normal friends, like Charlie had always told me I should do. I could set a goal: like, once I made a million dollars, I'd retire. I would keep my head together.

One Year Later
REESE

One guy was fucking my cunt and the other guy was fucking my asshole, but I couldn't feel anything at all.

I closed my eyes and tried to narrow my focus. There was a kind of burning stretching sensation at my genitals, but it seemed far away. I tried concentrating all my attention on the thin strip of flesh between my asshole and my vagina.

With a grunt, the guy fucking my ass finished and then, so close it was always laughably homoerotic, the guy fucking my cunt came. They pulled out slowly, dicks in hand. I saw, with relief, that they were both wearing condoms. The fact that I had made them use condoms seemed to signify I still had some instincts of self-preservation.

I hobbled over to the chair where I had left my clothes, and quickly got dressed. The guys were panting, still waking up from their almost infantile state of dumb pleasure. I didn't look at them—looking too long always made me want to hurt someone, although of course I hadn't brought a weapon with me.

It was one of the compromises I had made with myself. Since avoiding the bars entirely had proven an impossible task, I allowed myself a couple of visits a month. But I had decided I couldn't go to the bars when I was out of town on a job. And when I went out in LA, I couldn't bring a weapon with me. I didn't like how exposed being unarmed made me feel, especially afterwards, but those were The Rules.

I grabbed my jacket and got out of there before the guys had time to say anything.

I stepped out onto the front walkway of a shitty apartment complex. It was dark, but I had no idea what time it was. I could see my car parked on the street. These days, I was driving a Chevrolet SS, the same type of vehicle I'd used for my first job, with Cliff. Seeing it made me feel a little better.

Inside the car, I locked the doors, then looked back to the apartment complex. No one was following me.

My head was pounding from tequila shots and there was a bad taste in my mouth. As I sat, I felt something liquid seep into my underwear. It couldn't be cum—maybe it was lubricant from the condoms? Blood? Liquid shit? It didn't really matter.

I forced myself to pull down the sun visor and look at myself in the mirror. It was an alarming sight.

I took a breath. I had to go home, pull myself together. I was leaving town for a job the next day.

· · · ·

I started to feel better on the flight out of LAX. My asshole was sore—when I'd gotten home the night before, I'd discovered the liquid in my underwear was in fact blood, though there wasn't that much of it. But I was drinking a plastic cup of sparkling wine and my hangover was subsiding. Flying out of LA made me feel like I was leaving all my bad decisions behind.

I reminded myself that I had not broken The Rules. I had continued to refrain from killing anyone I wasn't meant to, and that was a little victory. I didn't feel like I was making Great Choices—I doubted Charlie would approve—but it seemed that I had to fuck up a little in order to be generally well-behaved.

In the evening, I would spend the night at a hotel, then begin my stakeout the following day. By then, I might be feeling totally recovered.

· · · ·

My flights took me from LAX to Dallas to Fort Meyers, where I picked up my rental car—an Audi RS3—and then drove to my hotel in Naples, Florida.

I was staying in a nice hotel, as I always did these days when I was on a job. It had a big, open lobby, with a bubbling water feature and lots of tropical plants. The lobby wasn't air-conditioned—it was warm and muggy and made me feel like I was still outside. I saw a small cockroach scuttle up the faux-stone wall. The wildness made my heart leap. I loved this hotel. I loved that cockroach.

My hotel room had cool tile floors, a large bathtub as well as a shower, a king-sized bed, and a minibar.

I opened the minibar and took out a Heineken—not drinking liquor on the job was one of The Rules. I started to undress, and realized I could pull my jeans straight off without unbuttoning the fly. I looked at myself in the full-length mirror.

I'd always been thin but now I was thinner. The mirror looked at me and said *kneebones, kneebones.*

How did I lose weight? I thought. *I eat all the time. Don't I?*

I sat on the bed and Googled stomach parasites, but nothing helpful turned up. I decided I'd have to buy some new pants.

I pulled out my phone, opened Facebook, and searched for Doug.

He had posted a new photo since the last time I had checked. It was of him, with both of his children under his arms. It seemed like he'd snatched them for the photo—one was a blur and the other was laughing hard. The photo was taken outside and it looked like a warm day—Doug was wearing a t-shirt, and I could see blots of moisture at the armpits of his shirt. I tried to imagine the smell of his sweat. I wondered if his wife took the picture.

I put my phone down. I pulled the curtains closed and turned off the lights. I climbed under the sheets. I left the barely-drunk Heineken by the minibar. That was a kind of progress, wasn't it?

I thought about the pies at the restaurant where I used to work, when I was young and poor. It was a chain restaurant that specialized in pies.

We sold 26 kinds of pies. They were divided into five categories: cream pies, specialty pies, fruit pies, seasonal fresh fruit pies, and cheesecakes. Except we never had seasonal fresh fruit pies available, so it was really four categories.

The cream pies category included lemon meringue, chocolate cream, banana cream, coconut cream, German chocolate, double cream lemon, double cream blueberry, and custard. Lemon meringue was contradictorily one of the worst-tasting and best-selling pies. I don't really like bananas or cream pies but taking a bite of cold banana cream pie would give me a strange, voluptuous thrill.

The specialty pies category included key lime, pecan, chocolate satin, cream cheese, lemon cream cheese, and Kahlua cream cheese. I believed all the pies in this category could have been moved to either the cream pie or cheesecakes categories, except for the pecan pie. But I was grateful for the pecan pie. It was the one genuinely good pie in the whole restaurant. It restored my faith when I despaired of all the other pies.

Fruit pies were the largest category and included apple, cherry, French apple, peach, pumpkin, razzleberry, rhubarb, sour cream apple, no sugar added apple, and no sugar added razzleberry. Other than the no sugar added pies, each of the pies in this group was syrupy and too-sweet. I tasted those pies and wondered why people ate pies.

The no sugar added pies were, remarkably, even worse. They tasted bland and flat and like they were aspiring to something they could not reach. They did what I thought impossible—they made the regular fruit pies taste good. At least *they* knew what they were meant to be.

The cheesecakes category included only caramel apple New York cheesecake and traditional New York-Style cheesecake. The traditional New York-Style cheesecake was not bad.

I didn't know why I wasn't asleep yet. I needed to be alert for the following day.

I remembered the airline attendant from the flight into Southern Florida. When we were boarding the plane, the line stalled and I had set my bag down on one of the seats in first class. Immediately, the attendant appeared and asked to see my ticket.

"This is not your seat," she spat. "You're sitting all the way back there."

And then she had snatched my bag off the seat and pushed it into my hands.

I was momentarily rendered speechless, and had silently followed the line of passengers to the back of the plane.

I had forgotten the interaction until this moment. I wondered how hard it would be to track down the attendant. It would probably not be easy. I didn't even know her name.

Wouldn't it be a funny surprise if it turned out she was the job I had been sent here to do? Would she remember my face when I showed up at her front door or outside her car, or wherever? What would she say to try and stop me, just before I blew her brains out the back of her head?

I drifted into sleep.

· · · ·

I picked up the dossier and my weapon the next morning.

The mark was a 36-year-old Chinese-American man named David Zhang, in town for an executive retreat at a nearby hotel. I followed him for a couple days as he went to different, equally ridiculous, company events. I watched him participate in a sand-sculpting workshop, watched him make fish tacos during a cooking class, and watched him disappear into a conference room for a brainstorming session. I watched him drink beers at a luau on the beach, watched him participate in a scavenger hunt, and watched him and his colleagues go out on a small boat that played a constant loop of Jimmy Buffet songs from its small speaker.

The mark was younger and a little hipper than most of the attendees—he wore dark blue jeans and v-neck t-shirts, while the rest of them mostly wore khakis and polo shirts. I wasn't entirely sure what he did for a living, since I hadn't read the dossier that thoroughly. It wasn't necessary—he was essentially a mouse in a cage at this point.

On the third night, I sat at the hotel bar and watched David Zhang, who was sitting at one of the tables on the other side of the bar. He was talking to a curly-haired woman who was also attending the retreat. I couldn't hear what he was saying, but it looked like he was trying to pick her up. He kept reaching his hand out toward hers, but not quite touching it. The look on her face said *maybe*. But then another woman came by and started talking to them, and after a moment, the curly-haired woman left the table with her. I saw the disappointment move across David Zhang's face.

He left the table and walked across the lobby. I stayed in my seat, and watched him disappear into the elevator, headed up. My heart rate accelerated. There were no cameras in the guest room hallways of this hotel. I waited for a few minutes, and then walked to the elevator. I got inside and pressed the button for the seventh floor.

Outside the door to David Zhang's room, I readied my weapon. He would think it was the curly-haired woman, I felt certain. I knocked on the door.

Yes? I heard a voice say. Then silence. Then with a click, the door opened a crack. I kicked it wide open, and David Zhang fell back onto the floor with a cry.

Hey! he said, and I shot him in the head. The door clicked closed behind me.

I'd done it clean and easy, in-keeping with The Rules. Well done me. I felt that little sink in my chest at how easy it was to kill a person, but I was used to that feeling. And that feeling, I reminded myself, meant I had done my job. The mark should never know what was coming. It *should* seem too easy.

I peered at the body. He did have nice clothes. And he wore a small size.

I considered. It wouldn't be easy removing jeans off a corpse. And not touching the body was also one of The Rules. But then I thought to open the drawers of the hotel dresser, where I found three pairs of neatly folded jeans. I took them, along with a couple of plain, soft-looking black t-shirts.

· · · ·

On the flight back to LA, I had a layover in O'Hare. I bought a Chicago Dog and ate it slowly, with a cold beer in a plastic cup.

I was doing fine.

· · · ·

I was staying in another shitty motel in Los Angeles but this one was, at least, close to the beach.

Charlie had encouraged me to rent a decent apartment, but he didn't press it. I think he understood that the nicer the place I called home, the more likely I was to want to flee it.

This place was OK, anyway—it was on the first floor and had a built-in kitchenette and a fenced-in private patio where I could smoke. It suited me.

I hadn't managed to make any friends or find anything significant to do with my free time when I wasn't working, but I hadn't made any serious Bad Choices like I had in Georgia with not-Doug and then the bartender. I had created a system that could contain me. I had even stopped imagining my own death.

And then I got the phone call.

Hey kid, he said. *It's Charlie.*

I froze. Charlie hadn't called me since after what had happened in Georgia. This couldn't be a good sign.

I just wanted to let you know, Cliff isn't going to be calling you anymore, he said.

What? I said. *Why not?*

Don't worry about it. A fellow named Patrick will be making the calls after this.

Is Cliff ok? I asked.

There was silence. Clearly it wasn't an acceptable question.

Anyway, you can pack a bag, Charlie said. *Book a flight for Pittsburgh tomorrow.*

He hung up the phone and I turned to ice.

Pittsburgh was where Doug lived. Pittsburgh was the dream I told myself as I fell asleep at night. Pittsburgh had become a kind of prayer to me, not a real place. I was terrified of going there.

How could I explain to Charlie that I couldn't go?

Saying no to Charlie wasn't an option. I did not want to discover what lay beneath Charlie's generous indulgence of me.

But why was he cutting off my contact with Cliff? Had I done something? Had Cliff? Or had something happened to Cliff?

I got out my phone and started reading through the crime reports, to see if any unknown man had been killed or injured during a violent attack, but I didn't find anything promising. I called a few hospitals, but no one would try and help me locate a middle-aged man with short gray hair and no known last name. Then I started to comb through the LA arrest records, and I found him. There was a mugshot of Cliff, though the blankly mean look on his face was unfamiliar to me. The name under the picture read Benjamin Owens. The charges were Burglary, Armed Assault, Unlawful Carrying of a Weapon, and Trespassing.

He must have been arrested on a hit. I didn't even know Cliff still carried out hits on his own—I just assumed he mostly trained new recruits. I wondered how long he'd be in jail. I thought of the family he'd mentioned. I felt relieved—and guilty over my relief—that it seemed to have nothing to do with me.

But there was still the problem of Pittsburgh. I would have to think of it like any other job. I would find out the name of the mark's neighborhood—let's say Pleasant Valley—and then I would tell myself I was visiting Pleasant Valley and I would think only of Pleasant Valley and it wouldn't be like I was in Pittsburgh at all. I would drink no liquor. I would not allow myself to hesitate before completing the hit. I would be in and then I would be out. Cliff would be proud.

I booked the flight to Pittsburgh and flew out the next day.

I picked up the rental car, the dossier, and my weapon, then drove to my hotel, which was near the airport.

The mark's name was John Alman and he was fifty-nine years old. He lived alone in a house he rented. The neighborhood was called Bon Air.

The dossier included details about his schedule and personal life, though there wasn't much to either. Other than a weekly trip to the grocery store, and an upcoming dentist appointment, John Alman seemed to do little but go to work and stay at home.

I felt nothing as I looked through the dossier, but when I put it down, a black despair fell over me.

Some part of me had thought I would open the dossier and find Doug in there. It would include all the information I had already gleaned about his wife, his children, and his job. Just the fact of it being in my possession would be a kind of death sentence for Doug.

I had to shake it off. Bon Air. I was going to a place called Bon Air to kill a mark named John Alman. It was just like any other job.

I drove to a chain family restaurant near the hotel, where I ordered mozzarella sticks and an Oreo milkshake, but I found I wasn't hungry. I wondered where Cliff was—if he was locked in a cell right now. I returned to my hotel and slept fitfully.

In the morning, I drove to John Alman's house in Bon Air. It was a narrow two-story gray clapboard house, streaked with grime, with no front yard to speak of. I parked and waited. At 8:40am, John Alman stepped outside his house, just as the dossier had predicted. He was a slight man with gray thinning hair. His body was small and unremarkable in a cheap short-sleeved button-down shirt and navy slacks, but he had something of a hobgoblin look about his face—his eyes, nose, and lips were all too big for his head.

I watched him get behind the wheel of his twenty-year old Toyota Camry, and then followed him to his work at a nearby office building.

I waited.

At 5:04pm, John Alman appeared again. I followed him as he returned home. He parked in the same spot, and then returned to his house.

I waited to see if he would reemerge. It was hard to imagine John Alman making an impact on anyone's life, let alone causing someone to want to kill him. He clearly didn't have any money and he didn't seem like someone who could send another person into a rage. I felt a deep, unsettling suspicion that this hit was some kind of message meant for me, especially since it had come from Charlie. But what could it *mean*?

I did my best to dismiss the thought. I waited until midnight with no sight of John Alman, and then returned to my hotel.

I knew I should eat something, but I wasn't hungry. I brought meal replacement bars with me on the stakeouts these days, but more and more often, I left them untouched. Perhaps there should be something in The Rules about regular meals? I picked up my phone and opened Doug's Facebook page.

There were no new posts—only the same one I had already seen, a photo of a grill full of cooking meat. Such a stupid fucking thing to post online. I opened a new window and searched Pittsburgh's White Pages for the name Doug Aldi. Only one result came up. It included an address. I put down my phone and got ready for bed.

. . . .

I woke early in the morning and lay in bed, staring at the ceiling. I would go to John Alman's house in Bon Air, I thought. I would park a few houses down the street from his. I would watch him leave for work. At about 4:45pm I would break into his house, either by picking the lock or by forcing my way in through the partially-obscured side window. Then I would wait for him to come home, shoot him, and leave. I'd return to LA the following day.

I showered and got dressed. I put a pair of gloves in my pocket and my gun in my holster. I got into the rental car, and then I put the address into my phone. I drove to Doug's house.

He lived in a suburb that was nicer than John Alman's neighborhood, but not too fancy. Most of the houses looked to be built in the 70's or 80's and had green front yards. Doug and his family lived in a two-story house with a sloping yard and a narrow set of stairs leading from the sidewalk up to the front door.

I shouldn't have come to his house, of course. It was against The Rules. But then, I thought, maybe it was a smart choice after all. Maybe once I saw Doug's face, this ridiculous obsession could finally die. Then I would go and kill John Alman and never return to Pittsburgh again.

At 7:42am the door opened and Doug stepped out of the house. I stopped breathing.

Seeing him, it was laughable that I had thought not-Doug back in Acworth, Georgia looked anything like him. The real Doug was so much better-looking than I had remembered. He was tall and effortless, with an easy smile—he was laughing even now, saying something as he walked out the door. There was suddenly a flash of movement, and I watched as one child came tearing out of the house, then the other. They started running circles around the station wagon that was parked in the driveway.

Boys! I heard Doug call, laughing. *Vermin!* he yelled.

One of the kids made a howling sound, but didn't stop running.

Then the front door opened again. His wife stood there, smiling at them. In the photos I had seen, she had looked like a suburban housewife—the kind of mother-wife I'd assumed Doug would need to make an adult out of him. But at the moment she looked surprisingly young and cool, in some kind of band t-shirt and skinny jeans. She held out a brown paper bag and raised her eyebrows.

Doug ran up the steps to the front door and swept her up in his arms. She cried, *put me down*, but she laughed and laughed. Finally, Doug set her down, snatched the paper bag from her hands, and planted a kiss on her mouth.

Then he turned and yelled, *Children! Into the Storm Chaser!* The kids froze, and then went tumbling into the backseat of the car. Doug blew a kiss to his wife, got into the car, backed it down the driveway, and drove away.

I had imagined I would try and have some kind of contact with him. Let him at least see me, even if we didn't speak. But I saw that his life was totally filled up. There wasn't room to add a sliver of another thing.

• • • •

I broke into John Alman's house easily.

I took a seat at the cheap laminate dining table and waited.

At 5:18pm, I heard him drive up. I heard the car door shut, and I heard him walk up the drive. My gun was in my hand. I heard him unlock the door, then close it and lock it behind him. He stepped into view, but he didn't see me. He was scratching his cheek, thinking about something. I could shoot him, but I didn't. I lowered the gun under the table, out of sight.

Hello John, I said.

He startled, and cried, *Jesus! Who are you?*

I'm Reese, I said.

What are you doing here? he said. *Did you break into my house?* His voice was surprisingly nasal. I realized I'd never heard it before.

Yes, I did, I said. *Sit down at the table.*

He glanced toward the kitchen, as if looking to see if I had an accomplice, or else maybe hoping there was someone in there who could save him. When no one appeared, he made his way to the table and sat across from me.

What do you want? he said in a small voice.

I came here to kill you, I said.

Kill me? he repeated, and his voice rose a pitch. Then he made a little laughing noise. He said, *Is this a joke?*

I lifted the gun above the table, aiming it at him.

It's not a joke, I said.

At the sight of the gun he abruptly slammed his hands on the table, as if preparing to leap up and run away.

Stay in the chair! I commanded.

His body made a kind of spasm, but he stayed seated. With his hands still pressed against the table, he started to rock back and forth. *Please*, he said. *Please don't kill me.*

I watched him rocking in his chair, his large eyes bulging, his fine gray hair sticking to the sweat on his face.

Why not? I said, coolly. *Why shouldn't I kill you?*

His lips made shapes, but it took a moment for him to find any words. Finally, he cried, *Because I want to live!*

I looked at him, hard. *Do you want to live?* I said. *Or are you just afraid to die?*

I want to live! he yelled. *I want to live!* He started rocking harder now, as if he could convince me through the force of his movement.

I got up from the table and moved to stand over him, my gun pointed at his head.

Why do you want to live, John? I've seen how you spend your days. You've got no friends, no family, not even a goddamn pet. You do nothing. You mean nothing. So why do you want to live?

Please, he said. He started to cry, and the rocking slowed. *I just, I just want to live.*

Tell me one thing. Tell me one single thing you have to live for, I said.

*I...I...*he stammered. *I have a sister in Scranton.*

I looked at him, and then I started to laugh. After a moment, he let out a shaky little laugh. Then he exhaled in relief.

I shot him in the temple. The force of the bullet knocked him off the chair.

I walked into his kitchen and opened his fridge. There was nothing appealing inside—condiments, some ground beef, a bag of whitish-red tomatoes. His cupboards were mostly empty, except for some boxes of dried pasta and cans of tuna fish and black beans.

It made me sad, looking at the canned beans. Of course, there was nothing John Alman could have said that would have stopped me. I might have broken The Rules by having a conversation with him, but I would never do something so reckless as letting him live. But while I hadn't meant to be cruel, it had felt cruel, dragging out his death like that. Still, I had hoped for something—some insight to come from him in his last moments. Why? I had attempted these kinds of conversations before I had Gotten My Shit Together, and it had been unwise. It had led, in some way, to the Bad Choices in Georgia.

Maybe, I thought, I was going about it the wrong way. John Alman had been terrified. Of course he hadn't been capable of profundity. If I really wanted to get to the heart of a person, I couldn't just point a gun at them and demand insight. I'd have to keep them captive for a long time, slowly break down their walls, force them to confront all their own fears and desires, and then extract their truths.

But truthfully, I reflected, I wouldn't be any good at that. It wasn't my skill set. All I really had going for me was the Killing Instinct. And besides, gleaning insight was not my job. I couldn't forget I was here to Do a Job.

I spotted a box of a generic brand of pecan sandies at the top of the cupboard. I pulled them down, wedged them under my arm, and left John Alman's house.

• • • •

On the way back to my hotel, I pulled into the parking lot of a liquor store. Not drinking liquor on the job was, of course, one of The Rules. But I had already broken one. Maybe The Rules were changing. Maybe I needed to trust all my instincts. I went into the store and left with a bottle of whiskey. I took a swig of it in the car, lit a cigarette, and drove back to my hotel.

• • • •

In the morning, I drove to Doug's house. I watched as he and his kids left together. An hour later, I watched his wife leave.

I walked up the stairs to his house. I had seen his wife lock the front door, so I immediately headed to the back of the house.

The backyard had a big flat expanse of somewhat unkempt grass, several large shady trees, and a small patio. The neighboring houses were pretty far away—a neighbor would have to be looking hard to get a good view into their yard.

I looked around. There was kid stuff everywhere—tricycles and bikes of different sizes, action figures and toy cars littered on the lawn and patio, and several pool toys lying half-deflated on the grass, though there was no pool. There was a cheap-looking patio table with mismatched chairs, and a big grill. I took out my latex gloves and put them on. I tried the patio door. It was locked with a simple mechanism that I broke with a couple of forceful pushes. I stepped inside, then slid the door closed behind me. Once closed, you could barely tell it was broken.

The house had a kind of dated quality. There was wall-to-wall beige carpeting and everything looked mass-produced—from the big overstuffed couches, to the highly varnished dining table, to the matching framed prints on the wall.

The house wasn't exactly dirty, but there were toys everywhere, and there were some stains on the carpet and walls that looked like they'd never come out.

I walked into the kitchen, which had ugly cherry wood-colored cabinets. I opened the fridge. It was packed full of loaves of bread, lunchmeats, cheese, a whole chicken wrapped in plastic, opened jars of pasta sauce, small containers of yogurt, bags of oranges and apples, juice boxes, canned soda, and beer. I closed the door.

I walked through every room of the house—the living room, the dining room, the laundry room, and the bathroom on the main floor, and then upstairs to the children's bedroom, the upstairs bathroom and, finally, the master bedroom.

There was a queen-sized bed with a peach-colored bedspread, matching end tables with lamps, and two dressers. One of the dressers was short and wide and had nothing on top. The other was taller and narrow and had a purple candle and a jewelry box on top. I went to that one first.

I opened the top drawer and found a pile of underwear and bars, all thrown together. I picked up a lavender colored bra. The tag was a little frayed and said Victoria's Secret, 32B.

I let the bra fall back into the drawer, then closed it. I suddenly felt very tired. I didn't even want to look in Doug's dresser, which was the treat I'd been saving for myself.

I opened the closet door. The closet extended to the right, far beyond the door. On the left side of the closet rod there was a short row of men's clothes—mostly jackets and a couple pairs of dress pants. The rest of the closet was filled with women's clothing.

I got inside and closed the door behind me. I climbed over shoes until I reached the far end of the closet. At the end were a couple of long silky robes. I sank into a seated position in the far corner of the closet, then moved the robes so that they shielded me entirely from view.

And then I waited. I waited for many hours, so many that I had to get up and pee in the middle of the day. I had my gun in my hand the whole time, certain I was going to be caught on the toilet with my pants around my ankles.

And then I returned to the closet to continue waiting.

Finally, in the late afternoon, I heard the sound of the door open, then the laughing shrieks of the children, followed by Doug's booming voice yelling after them. I listened to them play some kind of game—wrestling maybe—that involved a lot of laughing and yelling and loud thumping sounds, and ended with one of the children crying as Doug said, *I'm so sorry, buddy.*

I heard the wife come home a few hours later, and listened to Doug and the children greet her with wild excitement. I heard the rumbles of Doug and his wife talking, and heard the children come upstairs, into the room next to the one I was in, to play and yell some more. I heard the sounds of food being prepared, and then I heard Doug call to his children to come down for dinner. I heard the scraping sounds of food being eaten off plates, and then I heard the sounds of dishes being washed.

After that, it went quiet for a while, and all I could hear was the muffled sound of a television, and a few punctuating laughs. Then I heard multiple footsteps of people entering the upstairs bathroom, the sounds of running water and laughing, and then Doug's wife's murmuring voice and more pattering footsteps as they moved into the children's bedroom. After a while, I heard someone go back downstairs, and then heard the far-off sounds of the TV again. Finally, I heard two sets of footsteps climbing the stairs.

I heard them enter the master bedroom for the first time.

You're the one who swore you'd never use that tent again, I heard Doug's wife say.

I don't think I swore *I'd never use it*, Doug said.

You did, she said, laughing. *I remember you saying to me, I swear to God, I'm never using that tent again.*

Well that's probably because it rained that weekend. I seriously doubt it's going to rain this weekend.

Honey, you do what you like, the wife said. Her voice was getting nearer to me. *It's you and the boys who will be getting wet.*

The closet door opened. I could see light shining through the robes and I felt terribly exposed. My heartbeat seemed deafeningly loud. I didn't move. She had no reason to suspect anyone was in the closet, I reminded myself. My hand gripped my gun.

I heard her take down a hanger, then after a minute put it back.

Doug had said something to her, but I'd missed it. Finally, the closet door closed. I allowed myself to exhale.

I kept expecting the closet door to fly back open and Doug would charge to the corner of the closet, push back the robes, and find me crouched there. And then what? Would he laugh? Kick the shit out of me? Shake his head in disappointment?

But the closet door didn't open. I heard a faint squeak and imagined they had gotten into bed. I heard the sound of low voices, and then I heard Doug's wife laugh and cry, *Doug, Doug, get off me, you're so heavy!*

I heard his low laugh and I wondered if they were going to have sex. What would that sound like? How long would it last? But all I heard after that was Doug laughing and apologizing, then low murmurs, and then nothing at all.

From under the closet door, I could see the lights go out. I waited, listening. Finally, I heard the soft wheeze of Doug's breathing. I waited longer. I couldn't hear his wife breathing, but that didn't mean anything. Doug was just a noisy breather.

I stood up slowly, letting the feeling come back into my legs. I turned the safety on my weapon off. I stepped very carefully over the shoes to the closet door. I turned the handle as gently as I could, but couldn't stop it from clicking. I waited, holding my breath, but I heard nothing from the bedroom. I opened the closet door, then quickly stepped out, my gun aimed.

No one moved. I could see two figures in the bed, covered by the duvet. Now I could hear them both breathing.

I walked to the side of the bed where the larger figure slept. Doug first. I wouldn't risk him witnessing the rest.

When I got close, I saw he was facing me. Fast asleep. I raised my gun and shot him in the forehead. The gun made the clacking noise of a bullet being fired through a suppressor.

I heard an inhalation of air and I looked past Doug to his wife. She was facing away from me. I aimed and shot her in the back of the head.

I left the master bedroom and opened the door to the bedroom across the hall. I stood over the older child's bed, and shot him in the head. Then I walked to the younger child's crib. He was lying down, but his eyes were open. He was staring at me, curious and unknowing as an animal. Something in my chest lurched. I shot him in the forehead.

Everything was silent, the pounding in my ears gone.

I went back to the bedroom. The figures on the bed lay still. I went over to Doug's side of the bed. Other than the hole in his forehead, he looked peaceful. I carefully nudged him onto his back. Then I climbed onto the bed, and lay on top of Doug's body, resting my head on his chest. His body was still warm. I slept.

• • • •

I don't know how long I stayed there. I woke in the dark and had to pee, then returned to Doug's body. I woke again and it was light out. I wished to no one that the next time I fell asleep, I wouldn't wake up.

But again I slept and again I woke. Doug's body had gone cold. I didn't seem to have the will to shoot myself in the head like I ought to have. I decided to wait for the police. I rested my head on Doug's chest again.

But I couldn't fall back asleep. I looked up at Doug and his face had changed somehow. Slackened. I realized I didn't know him at all.

. . . .

On the flight back home, the waves started.

I hadn't felt them in a long time, and I closed my eyes, helpless. The lavender bra. The silken robe brushing against my knees. The younger child's big open eyes.

I sat and waited, but the images didn't stop. John Alman rocking in his chair. The light under the closet door. The kids racing a circle around the station wagon.

I was losing it. I was losing it. I was losing control. I had made too many Bad Choices and now I'd gone too far and I would never make my way back.

I grabbed the flight attendant's skirt as she passed me and asked for a whiskey. I drank through the rest of the flight.

On the way to my motel, I had the cab driver stop at a liquor store, and I picked up five bottles of whiskey. I opened one of the bottles on the drive home, over the cab driver's protestations, and drank deeply. Finally, I arrived back at my motel, where I locked the door, closed the curtains, and sank into bed.

. . . .

I drank. I drank for days.

Often I lay in my bed in a terror, overcome and weeping. Images I thought I had forgotten came back to me, of body parts, of faces in shock, of my victims shopping for groceries or putting gas in their cars.

I tried to imagine Cliff sitting at the end of my bed, giving me some advice that would brace me up and pull me back together. But the mirage of Cliff I conjured was wordless and faceless, and could tell me nothing.

Sometimes I tried to tear apart my own flesh, but I only left long red claw marks on my skin. I screamed into my pillow until my throat was raw.

And then sometimes, when I'd drunk enough whiskey to dissolve all the images playing across my mind, I thought of the time in Georgia, when Troy's hot blood had covered my body as he died. The thought excited me. I wanted to bathe in blood. I wanted to bathe in a pool so large that I could be completely submerged in blood. It would fill the gaps between my toes, gently fill my vagina and the crease under my ass, fill my bellybutton and my ears and nose, and cover every inch of my skin. I would open my lips and let it fill my insides.

At those moments, I felt powerful, erotic, and all-knowing. I felt I only had to unleash myself to be free.

· · · ·

I woke up to the sound of knocking on my door. It was light outside, but I didn't know if it was morning or afternoon, or what day it was. I was still wearing the clothes I had worn to Doug's house. I was surrounded by mostly-empty bottles.

I staggered to the door.

Jesus, Charlie said when I opened it.

We sat on the little patio that opened off my room because Charlie said the room stank.

Is it OK if I smoke? I asked.

Charlie sighed. *You don't need my permission to smoke,* he said.

I lit a cigarette.

A family of four, killed in their home, Charlie said. *The children were aged three and five, the wife thirty, husband thirty-three. His name was Doug Aldi. Your ex-boyfriend.*

How did he always know everything?

You know, I don't tell you what to do in your personal life, he said. *I don't consider that any of my business. But I would have thought it would go without saying that I cannot tolerate you engaging in highly illegal activities, such as murder. Especially the murder of someone with whom you have a known personal connection. It is incredibly reckless.*

I nodded.

Worse than that, it shows a troubling lack of judgment. I was worried about you after that ugly scene in Acworth. But I was willing to give you another chance because you've been such a professional otherwise. And I was glad to see you never repeated that kind of behavior. But now this? I am starting to seriously question your decision-making abilities.

I couldn't speak. I nodded again.

What happened to your weapon? he asked.

I returned it before I left Pittsburgh, I said.

And that's the weapon you used for…everything?

Yes, I said.

Well, at least there's that, Charlie said. He looked at me.

I want you to get your head together, he said, which made me think of the blown-apart smattering of brains I had once stuck my hands into. *I would say take some time off, but I think we both know what that leads to.* He gestured to the motel room, which I took to be both a reference to my drinking and to the murder of Doug and his family. *I'll get your next job lined up. In the meantime, get outside some time. Dry out. Get a hobby. Something that doesn't involve getting shitfaced and picking up strange men. You got it?*

I nodded again.

I like you, kid, I do. But I just can't tolerate this. That guy in Acworth was strike one. This thing, even though it was four innocent fucking people,

I'll call strike two. One more strike and it's...well, you gotta take that horse out and shoot it, you get it?

I didn't point out that he was mixing his metaphors. *I get it,* I said.

Good girl, Charlie said, and left.

From my chair on the patio, I could just reach a half-full bottle of whiskey. I dragged it to me, opened it, and took a long pull.

Could I possibly still be the functioning machine Charlie wanted me to be? Or was I to bathe in blood?

· · · ·

In the morning, I got into my car and started to drive.

He was surprised when the girl's car started slowing down. He had expected he would follow her all night and through the following day, and that he wouldn't have an opportunity to take her out until the evening. But only an hour or so after she left the convenience store, her car began to slow. He'd have thought she was getting off the freeway, but there was no upcoming exit in sight.

Then, as he watched, her car began veering off the road. What the hell was happening?

She drove slowly off the freeway, and finally came to a rolling stop on the shoulder.

He had a second to decide what to do. Maybe she was calling him out, trying to force him to reveal himself? If so, pulling over behind her would be playing right into her hands. Still, he felt fairly confident he would win in a standoff. He pulled off behind her and parked.

He waited, but no movement or noise came from her car. He didn't have to get out of his car, of course. But he wanted to end this thing. He drew his gun and slowly approached her vehicle. No shots came.

Finally, he reached her car. He crouched alongside it, weapon drawn, then slowly lifted his head, just behind the driver's window. She looked to be slumped over in the driver's seat. He opened the door and saw blood, black in the moonlight. There was a cheap pocketknife in her lap, and a large circle of blood soaking through her jeans. Both her wrists had long jagged cuts running up them.

His options flashed in front of him:

A. Leave her.

B. Shoot her in the head, then leave her.

C. ...

Fuck. He holstered his weapon, then took off his shirt and used it to tie up both her wrists. He reached under her, then lifted her in his arms. He carried her to his car, and settled her in the front seat. He touched his fingers to her neck. She was breathing and her heartbeat was faint, but regular. He wouldn't risk taking her to a hospital.

He got off at the first exit and pulled into the parking lot of a chain hotel. He quickly put on a shirt to cover his blood-stained undershirt, then went to the hotel lobby to get a room, where he made a laughing comment to the front desk clerk about his girlfriend having had a little too much to drink. When he returned to his car, she was still out cold. He grabbed the basic first aid kit from his trunk and his overnight bag, and then carried her up the stairs toward the room.

On the stairs, he glanced down and saw her eyes were slit open. She seemed to be looking at him, but after a moment, her eyes closed again.

Once they were in the room, he set her down in the bathtub. She groaned and lolled her head, but didn't open her eyes. He untied his shirt from her wrists. The cut on her right wrist was skinny and shallow, but the cut on her left wrist was much deeper and still bleeding. He cleaned the wounds, then dressed them with bandages and several layers of gauze. She lay limply in the tub. He reached over and removed the gun from her harness. Then he unlaced her boots and pulled them off.

He carried her to one of the beds, placed her between the clean white sheets, then pulled the covers back over her. He sat in the armchair next to the bed and looked at her. She was sleeping deeply now.

Was this the woman he'd been following for so long? She seemed so slight, so harmless. She'd hardly weighed a thing. She would have been so easy to crumple in his hand. And yet he hadn't. In a second, he had changed his life forever. It was probably the stupidest thing he'd ever done.

He turned on the television. He heard her moan and when he looked over, her eyes were open. She was looking at him, but he couldn't read her expression. He reached over and put his hand on her head. Her eyelids flickered, then closed. She slept.

· · · ·

She slept past ten in the morning. He'd showered and had just finished getting dressed in the bathroom when he heard a rustling sound from the room. He came out of the bathroom, and she leapt out of the bed. She reached into her jacket wildly.

If you're looking for your weapon, I have it, Zain said calmly.

You, she said. She looked at him, then at the room around them. Assessing the situation. *How long have you been following me?* she asked. Her voice was deeper than he'd expected. Steadier too.

Since LA.

How many days is that?

Six.

Fuck, she said. She stared at him. *You work for Charlie, then?*

Yeah, Zain said.

She looked down at the gauze on her wrists. *I need a cigarette*, she said.

· · · ·

They sat on the small balcony that was attached to the room. She smoked her cigarette in silence.

Finally, she looked at him and said, *Did he tell you to take me out?*

He might as well tell her the truth. *Not at first, no*, he said. *I was only supposed to follow you. Until last night.*

Last night, she repeated. *You went into that hotel room after I left?*

I did, he said.

You did. And then you called Charlie?

He nodded.

She looked at him steadily. She was brighter than he'd thought, more alert now that they were talking. *What happened last night, exactly?* she asked.

He told her about her driving off the road, and how he'd found her, slumped over the steering wheel.

So, she said, leaning back in her chair. *After Charlie told you to finish the hit, you found me in my car, passed out, bleeding all over the place, and you chose to take me in your arms, bandage me up and tuck me into bed?* She seemed genuinely amused.

Zain sighed.

Why? she asked.

I don't know, Zain said. *It was like coming across a puppy with a broken leg. I couldn't just shoot it.*

I think that's exactly the kind of situation where you're supposed to shoot the puppy, she said. *Or maybe that's horses.* She crushed her cigarette butt into the ashtray. *So what now? Did you patch me up just to take me out on the balcony of a Holiday Inn?*

No, Zain said.

No, she nodded. *Then what next?*

She looked at Zain. He shook his head. *You don't have a plan, do you?* she said.

It was the first time in a long time—maybe ever—that he had no plan. He was giving up everything he had been building, possibly his own life, and for what? He didn't know this woman. It wasn't his job to save her—and she didn't want to be saved anyway. And yet here they were.

No, he said. *I don't have a plan.*

What happened to my car?

I left in on the side of the road, he said. *It was the only option.*

It doesn't matter, she said. *But do you suppose there's somewhere around here I could get another pack of cigarettes?*

· · · ·

After what he considered a too-long stop at the convenience store, they drove to a small diner just off the freeway, where they sat in a booth facing each other.

It was strange seeing her up close. She had a light sprinkling of freckles across her nose and cheeks and her eyes were very dark, almost black. She had small teeth and sharply pointed incisors so that he saw a flash of fang when she smiled. Looking at her made him think she must have been fearsome at her peak.

You used to work for Charlie? he asked.

She nodded. She was poking at the stack of chocolate chip pancakes she had ordered.

For how long? he said.

I don't know, she shrugged. *Maybe a year and a half.*

You were on contract for him?

Yeah, she said. She dragged her fork across the pancake on the top of the stack.

What happened? You couldn't do it anymore? he asked.

She finally looked at him, with that acute black gaze. He wondered if he'd gone too far.

But she just shrugged again. *That wasn't it exactly.* She put her fork down. *Does he know where we are?*

I told him we were in Minnesota last night, so yeah, roughly. I destroyed the phone he used to use to contact me, and both the SIM cards I had with me. You didn't have a phone on you.

She shook her head. *It was in the car,* she said. Then she looked at him. *Wait, you destroyed your Charlie Phone?*

My what?

Nevermind, she said. *How long do you think before he sends someone after us?*

He'll be expecting me to call tonight, at the latest, Zain said. *So maybe tomorrow, maybe the day after that.*

Shall we just wait for his men to arrive, then? she asked, and smiled.

He looked at her, unsure if she was joking. *Is that what you want?* he asked.

No, she said. *I hate waiting.*

A plan started to form in his head. That was good. *We could head out together,* he said. *Go south, to the border. Then cross into Mexico. Do you have a passport?*

Not with me.

Ok, then, we get one made. It can't be that hard. Do you have money put aside? Any cash?

A couple hundred bucks, she said. *Most of my money is in the bank.*

Mine too. We'll have to withdraw as much cash as we can, get across the border, then lay low for a couple months.

A couple months?

Yeah, probably, he said. *Until our trail cools off. Then we can split up, go our separate ways.*

You wanna flee to Mexico with me for a couple months?

He felt a little silly when she put it that way. *Do you have a better idea?* he said.

She scratched her head, then looked under her fingernails. *I have been told, more than once, that I have a tendency to drive people crazy,* she said. *And all this passport stuff will slow you down. Maybe we should go our separate ways now.*

We could, Zain said. He probably *would* get away faster without her. And two people on their own would be harder to track than two people together. He looked at her. She'd resumed poking at her pancakes with her fork. *And what would you do?* he asked. *Keep driving all over the country, bringing strangers back to your hotel rooms, and crying when you can't get the pie you want?*

She looked up at that. *God, I keep forgetting you were following me for so long.* She shrugged. *Yeah, I guess that's what I'd do.*

Charlie would find you in no time, Zain pressed. *If you come with me, you'll stand a better chance.*

She stuck out her tongue and pressed it against the pointed tines of her fork. There was something slightly sexual in the gesture that Zain found unsettling.

Or, she said, *we could part ways now and you could finish out your job. Take me by surprise at some rest area later today. I'm sure you'd be successful. I don't even have a weapon.*

He shook his head.

No? she said.

No, he said.

Okay, then. I guess we better head to Mexico. You realize we're much closer to Canada, right?

Yes. But it's easier to disappear in Mexico. And we have a few days head start.

Sounds like we have a plan, she said.

• • • •

A few hours later, they had each withdrawn as much cash from their accounts as the bank would allow, picked up a cheap phone for her and some new SIM cards, and traded in Zain's vehicle for another at a fairly sketchy used car lot. Zain put half of his cash into his bag, and hid the other half in the new car's spare tire. Then he moved the first aid kit, the emergency vehicle kit, and the portable jump starter with jumper cables from his old car to the new one. And then they got on the road.

They didn't talk much at first. She leaned far back in the seat, chain smoking, while Zain drove south. When they stopped at a gas station, she bought two bags worth of crap, then asked if she could drive.

Once they were on the freeway, she looked over at him.

Can I ask you something? she said.

Sure.

You didn't know you were leaving town, right? That like, six days ago or whatever, I'd get in my car and start driving across the country? And you'd have to follow me?

No, I didn't know that, he said.

So then how do you have all these fancy dress shirts with you?

My shirts? he said, surprised. *They're not fancy.*

103

OK, so then how do you have all these not-that-fancy dress shirts with you?

I only have four, he said.

She kept staring at him.

I always have an overnight bag in my car, he said. *With a couple changes of clothes.*

Do you always have a first aid kit? she said.

Yes.

And an emergency car kit and a portable starter with jumper cables?

Those too, he said.

Well, she said, with a laughing note in her voice, *Aren't you prepared.*

They drove for hours. As it started to get dark, she said she could pull over in the next town and find a hotel for the night.

I was thinking we'd keep going until morning, Zain said. *I can drive.*

She didn't look at him, just stared straight ahead at the road. Her jaw was tight. Zain realized she was frightened.

Or we could pull over at the next town, Zain said. *It's not like anyone will be looking for us yet, and we might as well get some sleep.*

She nodded.

Zain did insist they stay at a decent hotel and got them a room with two beds and a balcony. He grabbed his bag while she rummaged around in the back seat until she found a bottle of whiskey, then followed him up to the room.

It's non-smoking, she called out as he put down his bag.

I know, he said. *There's a balcony.*

I like smoking in bed, she said, and exhaled in frustration. She opened the bottle of whiskey and took a long drink, then offered him the bottle.

No, thanks, he said. *Are you sure that's a good idea?*

Just keep me away from the bars. She opened the door to the balcony, then stepped out and lit a cigarette.

Do you want to order room service? he said. *We haven't eaten all day.*

I'm not hungry, she said, looking off the balcony.

You have to start eating, Zain said.

I eat all the time.

No, you don't. He approached the balcony and stood in the doorframe. She looked over at him. *You order three slices of pie and then you only take a bite of each one. You buy all this gas station crap and you never touch it again. You drink your dinner every night.* He nodded at the bottle in her hand.

She took a swig, slitting her eyes at him. *I can't believe that whole time, I never knew anyone was watching me. Just like any dumb fucking mark.*

Well, you didn't exactly seem like you were trying to get away with anything, he said.

Her face changed. *When you went into that motel room after me, what did it look like? Was it pretty bad?*

Yeah, Zain said. *It was pretty bad.*

Her eyes were dark and shining.

What happened? Zain asked. *Did he come after you or something?*

No, she said quietly. *He didn't come after me.* She looked up at him. *You should do it now*, she said.

What?

You should finish the job. It isn't too late. You can tell Charlie—well, tell him whatever, he'll forgive you because it'll be done.

No, Zain said.

You should have just let me die there, she said. *Charlie is right to make it happen. He's not punishing me or anything. He just knows. I'm like a broken piece of a machine and I can't be fixed.*

Tears fell on her face, and she quickly wiped them away.

Suddenly, she smiled.

Come on, she said. She reached over and placed a fingertip on the middle button of his shirt, just over his sternum. *I'll make it easy for you.*

I already said no, Zain said.

Because of the whole puppy thing? she said. *I'm not so defenseless now.*

Because I'm done with it.

You mean the job, everything? You're done for good?

Yes, he said. He knew the moment he said it that it was true.

She seemed to know, too. She dropped her hand from his shirt, gave him a crooked little smile, and shrugged.

I guess it's Mexico, then, she said.

• • • •

She agreed to let him re-dress her wounds, and sat in the bathtub while he unwrapped the gauze. The cut on her left wrist was still bleeding, but it didn't look infected. He reapplied ointment to her wrists, then carefully re-wrapped them in fresh bandages. She wanted to take a shower afterwards, but he told her that was impossible—she had to keep her bandages dry. She got out of the tub, took a long pull of whiskey, and walked back into the room. She stripped down to her t-shirt and a pair of black underwear, then got into her bed with a sigh.

He kept his back to her as he took off his shirt and hung it in the closet, and then took off his pants and hung them up too. In his undershirt and boxers, he walked to the nightstand on the far side of his bed, and laid down both of their weapons. He could feel her watching him. He got into his bed, then turned off the lights.

He lay in bed for a long time, staring at the ceiling. He could tell from her breathing that she was still awake too.

Finally, she said, *I can't sleep.*

Just close your eyes, Zain said.

The bed feels weird.

It's the nicest bed you've slept in since you left LA.

Yeah. That's why it's weird, she said.

Are your eyes closed?

I should have had more whiskey.

That won't help.

Fine, she said, and sighed.

After a moment, she said, *What's your name, anyway?*

Zain.

I'm Reese, she said.

I know.

· · · ·

In the morning, she got out of bed and, still in her t-shirt and underwear, immediately went to the balcony to smoke.

She didn't turn around as he got up, just stared out into the parking lot below. He glanced at the guns on the nightstand, and decided to leave them there. What was he afraid of? He didn't resemble a biker in the slightest.

He gathered a change of clothes and went into the bathroom to take a shower. When he came out, she instantly said, *I want to take a shower.*

You can't yet, he said. *You have to keep the bandages dry. Just give it a few more days until you stop bleeding.*

She made a grunt of frustration.

You wanna go get breakfast? Some real food? he asked. She just shrugged. He sighed and went to the nightstand. He put his weapon in his holster, and then put on his jacket.

Hey, he said, and held out her gun to her.

Light flickered in her eyes.

Yeah? she said. *Thanks.* She took the gun in her hand, lightly ran her thumb down the barrel, then tucked it into her holster.

Ok, she said. *Let's go eat a big motherfucking breakfast.*

· · · ·

They drove all day, taking turns driving, listening to small-town radio and smoking cigarettes. They went through a drive-through and Zain ordered them grilled chicken sandwiches. She put on a pair of pink sunglasses at a gas station, walked out wearing them, and didn't take them off for hours. At a different convenience store, she lingering in every aisle, gleefully filling her basket. For a second, staring down at the basket filled with sour candy, pink marshmallows, spicy pretzels, miniature sticks of salami, packaged brownies, a bottle of sparkling wine, toy bubbles, a plastic sheriff's badge, and a keyring attached to a tiny gold glittering kaleidoscope, he caught a fragment of her glee at buying all the pointless things you could possibly want. She caught the look on his face and laughed. *You smiled!* she cried. *I saw it!*

They made it to Fort Worth before it started to get dark, and they pulled over at a Comfort Inn.

In the room, still wearing the pink sunglasses, she opened a fresh bottle of whiskey and took a long drink. She held the bottle out to him.

Fine, he said, and took the bottle from her.

They sat on the hotel balcony, drinking and smoking.

You think we'll make it to Mexico tomorrow? she asked.

To the border, yeah. We'll find a place to stay in Laredo until we can cross over.

And then what?

I don't know, he said. *Head to a city we can get lost in.*

Sounds almost romantic when you say it like that, she said, teasingly.

Not the word I'd use, he said.

She was looking at him. *You're hard to get a read on, you know that?*

So I've been told.

I guess that must be good for the job, she said. *Never give anything away. Though of course, the second I saw you, I knew you had to work for Charlie.*

Why's that?

Those eyes, that face, those clothes. You look like a fucking painting. No one who looks like you would be hanging out at some shitty motel in Minnesota in the middle of the night.

Is that why you did what you did? he asked. He'd been wondering it since that night. *Because you knew I was coming after you?*

What, this? She lifted her wrists, and smiled a little. *No, I just wanted to die.*

They sat in silence for a moment.

How long have you worked for Charlie? she asked.

Eight years.

Eight years. You must be good at it.

Yeah, he said. *I was.*

You never felt like...like you were coming undone?

He looked at her, fidgeting with the strap of her gun holster. *Is that what happened to you?*

I don't know. Things just started getting fucked up in my head. The more fucked up they got, the more I tried to find a path out but...instead I just seemed to end up going deeper and deeper into it.

I never felt like that, no, he said. *I guess I just turned parts of myself off.*

Well, you have more self-control than me, she said. Then she sighed. *Zain,* she said. *I have to take a shower.*

Just wait a little longer, he said.

No, I've been thinking. I'll get into the shower and keep my arms up, well out of the water. Then you just, like, sponge me down.

You want me to bathe you? he said, incredulous.

Yeah. Come on. Before he could say anything, she had left the balcony and was heading toward the bathroom. He grabbed the bottle and took a long drink of whiskey, then followed her.

She was already undressing, topless and skinny in her underwear. Then she slipped the underwear off and climbed into the bathtub. She turned to him and lifted her arms with a flourish.

Turn the water on, she said.

He looked into her eyes, careful not to lower his gaze. Her stare was steady. *Fine,* he said.

He didn't want to get his shirt wet, but he didn't want to alarm her by removing his shirt, so he unbuttoned both his cuffs, then rolled them up to above the elbows. Then he reached over to the shower knobs. He could feel her body close to him, almost brushing against him.

You might want to step back, he said.

She didn't move.

It's going to be cold, he warned.

I know, she said, still not moving.

He turned on the hot and cold taps at the same time. The water shot onto her body, and she made a gasping sound, but still didn't move. She breathed hard, her small breasts rising high on her jutting ribs. And then she exhaled deeply. He could feel the heat coming off the water.

Is that too hot? he said.

I like it, she said. *Will you wash my hair?*

He opened the small bottle of shampoo and emptied some into his hands. She turned around and he worked the shampoo through her hair, then helped rinse it out as she leaned her head back into the water.

Now wash my body, she said, nodding at the packaged bar of soap on the sink.

Zain carefully opened the bar of soap, then rubbed it between his palms to make a lather. He started at her throat, and then worked his way down her arms, stopping to pick up the bar of soap and rub it between his palms again when he needed more. She stood very still, waiting for him to continue.

He ran his hands from her collarbones over her breasts. They felt warm and soft in his hands. He ran his hands over her ribs and her stomach, then over her hips. With her arms still lifted, she angled her armpits at him, which were dark and unshaved. He washed under her arms.

He rinsed off his hands while she ran her armpits under the water. Then she faced him again, like a challenge.

He rubbed the soap between his hands, then ran the lather over her hips. Her pubic hair was also dark and untrimmed. He looked at her. She raised her eyebrows. He gently ran his hand over the dark hair, rubbing the soap into it, and then ran his hand between her legs. He could feel the soft brush of her pussy under his fingers. He felt the reaction in his own body—the slightly stiffening cock, the beating heart—and did not react to the reaction. She didn't move at all.

He washed her thighs, and then couched down to wash her calves and ankles. He lifted one foot, thought of checking the hooves of a horse, then lifted the other foot. The soles of her feet were hard and callused.

Turn around, he said. She did and he washed her bottom and her back. He rinsed his hands under the water.

Now rinse off, he said, and she did. He watched the soap run off her body until she was rinsed clean. He felt he had survived something, somehow.

He turned off the water, then pulled down a towel, unfolded it, and wrapped it around her shoulders.

She was no longer staring her hard stare at him. She looked almost shy as she gathered the towel around herself. *Thank you*, she said.

No problem, he said.

· · · ·

The next day, they woke up to rain. Even though it was morning, the room was dark.

Her mood was morose. She only picked at her breakfast, then stared out the window at the rain as he drove. She smoked with the windows up, which irritated him, but he figured it was better than asking her not to smoke and watching her sulk further.

Where do you live when you're not working? she asked, staring out the window.

In LA, he said, though of course they both knew he couldn't go back.

Do you have a girlfriend? she asked.

He laughed. It had been a long time since anyone had asked him that question. *No*, he said. *Nothing like that.*

Do you have friends?

Sure, he said. *Some people I see now and then.*

Do they know what you do?

Of course not, he said.

What about your family?

I don't see my family, he said shortly.

No friends, no family, she said. *And now you're stuck with me.*

He looked over at her. She was smiling her fanged smile at him.

You want? She held up her cigarette. He gave a nod, but instead of giving him a cigarette, she reached out and held hers to his mouth. As he inhaled, her fingertips brushed against his lips. She took her hand away and he exhaled.

He looked at the road, which stretched out flat in front of them. He was a little ashamed of his reaction to her. He could feel it in his body, his desire. He didn't understand it—she wasn't very pretty, and wasn't anything like the type of women he'd been attracted to in the past.

Maybe he was just lonely. It had been a long time since anyone had touched him. At some point, he'd tired of casual encounters with women he met in bars, and he knew he was not going to pursue a relationship while he was still in this job.

He had learned long ago not to mistake the reactions of his body for what he really wanted. And yet his mind kept getting drawn back to the idea that there was some meaning in his desire, as if acting on it could make some kind of sense of this situation.

He didn't want her to think that this was why he had fished her out of the car—something as stupid as wanting to fuck her. And yet, for all her unpredictable wildness, he had the feeling she knew everything long before he did.

What was your first job? she asked suddenly.

It was a woman in LA.

A woman? Really?

He nodded.

How did you do it?

I was dumb about it. Cocky. I watched her for a couple days and then I just walked up and knocked on her door. I pretended to be her neighbor, told her I was starting a new neighborhood watch group and asked if I could come in and tell her about it.

Did she let you in?

She did.

And then what?

Then I shot her.

Jesus, she said. *That's impressive.*

It was stupid, he said. *Needlessly risky. She could have slammed the door in my face, and I'd have had a much harder time following her after that. Charlie pointed that out to me, of course, when I told him about it after.*

Was he mad at you?

Not exactly. He thought it was foolish, taking a risk like that. But he also saw I could think on my feet, and act when I needed to. I think he figured he could work with me.

What was her name? That first woman.

I don't know, he said. *It was a long time ago.*

You don't remember her name?

You remember all their names? he asked.

Yeah. Every one.

Well, I try and forget them as soon as it happens. I try and think it's like they weren't meant to be in the world anymore. So it's better to imagine they never were.

Is that, like, your philosophy? she asked in a teasing voice.

Something like that. Look, could you open a window? The car is full of smoke.

It's raining, she said in the same teasing voice.

Just crack it.

She pressed down on both the front window buttons, and rain immediately began pouring into the car.

Hey! he yelled, but she kept her fingers pressed down until both windows were completely rolled down. Rain sheeted through the windows. Within seconds, they were both soaked. She laughed and laughed.

· · · ·

They reached Laredo before it got dark. They drove through town, looking for a place to stay until they could cross the border.

Look! she cried out suddenly. *Can we stay there? Please?*

The hotel was bright pink. It was surrounded by a chain link fence and had a kidney-shaped swimming pool and several tall palm trees in the little courtyard. On one side of the hotel was a bar and on the other side was a fast-food restaurant, where a large group of teenagers were hanging out in the parking lot. It was not a nice hotel, but she'd compelled them both to stay in far worse.

Fine, he said.

She brought a few of her plastic bags of gas station junk into the room, while he peeled off a stack of bills from his stash, and left the rest of his things in the room. She promised to stay put while he went out to try and find someone who could create a fake passport in a short amount of time.

He walked a few streets down into the main part of town, then spent several hours sitting on barstools, having conversations that didn't lead anywhere.

He knew his urgency was probably scaring people off. He had too much of the whiff of a narc about him. Maybe, he thought, she should have done this job. With her shabby clothes and her irrepressible wolf grin, no one would mistake her for a cop.

Finally, he got to talking with a guy who said he could arrange it, and Zain agreed to meet him the following afternoon with half the money and two passport-sized photos.

It was late by the time he returned to the hotel. A little street market had sprung up, and he walked through a crowd of people and vendors selling grilled corn, cheap jewelry, and brightly-colored sliced fruit.

The hotel room was dark when he let himself in. She was leaning against the wall, facing the door, as if she'd been waiting for him. She was wearing one of his shirts—which was unbuttoned all the way down the front and just barely covered her breasts—a pair of black underwear, and nothing else. There was a cigarette in her hand.

I found someone who can make you a passport, he said.

OK, she said, and started to walk toward him. She didn't seem drunk, but her expression was strange, unreadable.

It's gonna be three thousand dollars. We need to get him a couple photos and the first half of the money tomorrow.

Sounds good, she said. She laid her hand on his chest and pressed lightly, walking him backwards, then pushed him down into the hotel chair. She stood her legs on either side of him, straddling him, then sat on his lap.

Reese, he said.

She took a bottle of whiskey off the table next to the chair, then took a drink. She handed the bottle to him.

Well, he'd already blown a hole in his life. He took a drink. Before he had even finished, she pulled the bottle away and kissed him. Whiskey ran down both their faces. For a moment, a part of him resisted, and then it didn't.

She crushed her cigarette into the ashtray, and then lay her fingers along his throat.

What was the name of the woman you killed? she whispered. *That first one.*

He swallowed. *Laura Stone,* he said.

She started to unbutton his shirt.

What did she look like?

He hesitated a moment, then said, *She had light brown hair, blue eyes. She was pretty.*

What did her body look like?

She—she had large breasts. A small waist. She dressed conservatively.

She finished unbuttoning his shirt and took it off of him, throwing it to the floor. *How did she look at you when she opened the door?*

Zain closed his eyes. He could see Laura Stone's face, smiling at him. *She looked happy to see me,* he said. *She looked at me like we already knew each other.*

She lifted off his undershirt, and threw it down. She ran her hands down his chest. *Did it seem like she wanted you?*

We didn't—

No, but. The way she looked at you, she said. *Did she look at you like she wanted to fuck you?*

I—yes, he managed to say. She unbuckled his belt, and then undid his pants.

And then she let you into her house. Where did she take you?

Into the living room. We sat on the couch.

She freed his cock. He was breathing hard. *And then what?*

Then we—we talked.

She pulled aside her underwear and slid her pussy down onto his cock. *And then what?*

Fuck, he gasped.

Then what? she said.

And then I said—I-

Yes? She started to rock her hips back and forth, pushing him deeper inside her.

I said, Laura, I came here to kill you.

Oh god, she said. She was touching herself as she rode his cock. *And then?* she said.

He opened her shirt, exposing her breasts. He ran his hands over her breasts, then took her hard nipples between his fingers.

Then I took out my gun, he said.

Oh god, she said again. He pinched her nipples.

I aimed it, he said.

Don't stop.

And I shot her in the head.

She came with a loud cry. Her pussy tightened around his cock and in a moment, he was coming inside of her.

He wrapped his arms around her to keep her close, close, close to him, to make the moment stretch on and on because he knew once it was over he would be sick with himself.

. . . .

She slept deeply, snoring lightly. But he lay awake most of the night, only falling asleep when it started to get light outside.

. . . .

When he woke up, she was sitting naked at the edge of the bed, studying the gauze on her wrists. She looked over at him as he sat up in bed. She stared levelly. He said nothing. She slowly unwrapped the gauze off one wrist, gathering it up in her fist. She glanced at him, then unwrapped the other wrist. She brandished her wrists at him. Both her wounds had started to scab over.

I'm going to take a shower, she said, then walked naked to the bathroom. For someone with so little regard for social niceties, she did like to stay clean.

He walked to the window, and pushed it open. He lit a cigarette. He had never smoked so much as he had in the past few days. Maybe this was his truest self: an empty, endlessly wanting person.

She came out of the shower dripping wet, a towel wrapped around her head. She started kicking at the pile of clothes on the floor.

I'm so sick of wearing this shit, she said. *Maybe we could go shopping for new clothes today, for Mexico. Do we have anything we have to do?*

We have to get your passport photo, but that's it.

Maybe I could dye my hair for the photo! We should try and change our look anyway, don't you think?

She looked in the mirror at herself. *Maybe I could dye it blonde?* She pulled the towel off and combed her wet hair with her hands. *Or black. Then we'd be like brother and sister.*

No, we wouldn't, he sighed.

She looked at him. *What's the matter with you?*

Nothing, he said. He knew that dipping into melancholy was the kind of thing she usually did. But he felt helpless against the dark feeling that was dragging him down.

She wrapped the towel around her body and walked to him. She took the cigarette from his fingers and used it to light one of her own.

What's the point in being upset when we're gonna die soon, anyway? she said.

In spite of himself, her flippant tone made me smile. *How do you figure?*

Even if we make it to Mexico, we'll still be tracked down. We'll have to take more money from our accounts at some point. The car we're driving isn't exactly untraceable, not if you can trace the car we exchanged for it. Your passport, I assume, is in your name. And we're still walking around with these faces. Charlie knows people everywhere. I don't know anyone. Do you know anyone?

The only person Zain ever knew like that was Charlie. *No,* he said.

Right. He knows cops and criminals and probably people who work border control. He'll track us down and send someone after us. Maybe a couple people. They'll be good at their jobs. We won't even know they're watching us until they're on top of us. Maybe we'll never know at all, and then it'll be over.

When did you decide to get a functioning brain? he said, then immediately regretted it. But she only shrugged.

I mean, it's easy enough to work it out, she said. *Since you refuse to complete this job, we just have to accept we're going to die soon. Which brings me to my original point, which is, who cares how we fuck, when we don't have that long to live anyway?*

Zain sighed.

What is it? she said. *You never wanted there to be any pleasure in the job?*

I never thought there was, Zain said.

She took his hand, the one not holding a cigarette, and lifted it to her lips. She stuck the first two fingers in her mouth. Instantly, he felt desire thrum in him. She sucked on the fingers, hard, and then slowly pulled them out of her mouth, licking his fingertips as she did.

Why not take your pleasure wherever you can? she said.

. . . .

Maybe it was delusional to think he could prevent Charlie from tracking them down, but he at least had to try. They checked out of the pink hotel, and then drove to a used car lot, where they sold the car they'd been driving for a lot less than it was worth. Then they went to another used car lot and bought a different car—they got a gray 2006 Mazdaspeed3 after she wouldn't shut up about how it was the perfect getaway car.

Zain drove them to a department store, where he bought Levi's and a few plain t-shirts to better blend in, and then they stopped at a drugstore so she could get her passport picture taken and buy more needless crap.

As they drove along a road near the border, looking for a hotel, she insisted they stop at a cheap touristy clothing shop, where she bought some tiny mini-skirts, t-shirts emblazoned with glittery images, a couple dresses, and a pair of spindly high heels.

The hotel they chose was a crumbling three-story orange edifice called Hotel Milagro. It was decidedly shittier than the last place, but it still had a pool. He kept an eye out behind them, but he was fairly certain no one was following them. Once they were settled into the new hotel, with the new car parked outside, he felt relieved. If nothing else, they'd hopefully bought themselves some time.

In their room at Hotel Milagro, she disappeared into the bathroom with one of her drugstore bags. She re-emerged some time later, naked, with all her body hair shaved off and her brown hair dyed jet black. She immediately tried to reach her hands into his pants, but he stopped her.

I have to go meet the guy about your passport now, he said.

She threw herself onto the bed and buried her face in the pillow.

Don't get into too much trouble while I'm gone, he said.

She made a sound into the pillow.

You'll be here when I get back?

She said nothing.

Hey, he said. *What do you want your name to be? On your new passport?*

At that, she lifted her head off the pillow. She grinned. *Laura Stone*, she said.

He sighed, shook his head, and left. He met the guy at the same bar, and handed over the cash and the passport photos. The guy told him he'd have the passport ready in three days, and that he'd collect the second half of the money then. Zain thought he seemed legit, but he didn't totally trust his instincts anymore. Still, he agreed to meet him in three days.

As he walked back to the hotel, he thought of the houseplants in his apartment in LA, which by now must be dying—shedding brown leaves in the sunny, empty rooms.

When he opened the door to the room, she leapt up to stand on the bed. She was wearing a black tank top with an image of bright pink lips across the breasts, a short black skirt, and the high heels. She had put on dark eye makeup and her newly black hair was in a tangle. She had her weapon holstered under her arm.

You look like a teenager, he said.

She laughed and leapt from the bed, into his arms.

Let's go out! she cried.

. . . .

They walked through the little street fair as the sun started to set, making their way past brightly-lit rides and games, through throngs of teenagers and families, and past vendors selling fried and sweet snacks.

They rode the Ferris wheel and ate cotton candy and hot fried churros and went to the little bar in the corner of the fair and drank tequila shots with lime wedges and salt.

When they left, she pulled him into an alley and kissed him. She put her lips to his ear and said, *Take me back to the motel.*

She was naked before he had even closed the door. He fucked her on the bed, holding her down by her wrists. She bit his lip, hard, and his blood mingled in their mouths. He came inside her and then went down on her, tasting his come and his blood and her cunt as she came against his mouth.

Afterward, she lay in his arms. He could feel her heart. The noises from the street outside came in through the open window—people shouting, kids laughing, an ambulance wailing. He looked down at her scalp, where the thin line of her part had been dyed an almost blue shade of black. He bent his neck and kissed the center of her scalp.

You awake? he said.

Mmm.

Maybe we don't have to die, he said. *Maybe we could make it to Mexico, and then find a little place to live on the beach. Just disappear.*

Shhh, she said softly. *You're dreaming.*

• • • •

In the morning, they had breakfast at a nearby diner, and then picked up some cheap bathing suits at the drugstore. They swam in the hotel pool all day, only getting out to eat lunch and to smoke cigarettes. In the evening, they ate tacos at a nearby taqueria and then played pool in a rough little bar down the street, drinking bottles of Mexican beer.

After she beat him at pool for the third time, she strolled to the bar and ordered them tequila shots. They licked salt off each other's hands, followed it with the tequila shots, and then sucked on lime wedges. She immediately ordered another round, then another. When she waved to the bartender for a fourth time, he said, *Maybe we should slow down.*

She gazed darkly at him, but said nothing. The bartender poured their shots. She didn't take her eyes off him as she lifted the glass and downed it in one go.

Look, he said. *I'm only trying to-*

Suddenly, she whirled around and walked out of the bar.

Goddammit, he muttered. He paid for their drinks, then left the bar. He didn't like being forced to follow her.

He quickly found her on the street. She was walking fast, back in the direction of the hotel.

Hey! he called. She kept walking. He hurried to catch up with her. When he was a couple feet away, he called out again. Still, she kept walking. Finally, he reached out and grabbed her arm, then spun her around. *Hey!*

For a moment, she looked furious, breathing hard and glaring at him. Then she started to laugh. *Go on then,* she said. *Rough me up.*

What the hell's going on? he said, letting go of her arm.

She took a step towards him. *What are you gonna do?* she said in a low, provoking voice.

He leaned down, grabbed hold of her legs, and stood up, so she fell over his shoulder. She screamed in laughter as he carried her back to the hotel.

In their room, he lightly tossed her onto the bed, then turned to fasten the many locks on the door. When he turned back around, she was walking toward him, smiling and dark.

She tilted her face up to his and he leaned down to kiss her. She pulled back and ran her hand down his chest, and then ran her finger along the inside of the waistband of his boxers. Then she reached for his gun, and slowly removed it from the holster. He thought she would put it down. Instead, she pointed it at his chest.

Don't do that, he said. She smiled. She lifted the gun and pointed it at his head.

Put the gun down, he said. He wasn't sure what she might do, but he knew enough to be scared. *I mean it, Reese*, he said.

She cocked her head. *That isn't my name.*

He looked at her. She was still smiling. She was playing some kind of game, but was it the kind of game that ended with a hole in his head?

Laura, he tried. She smiled wider, showing her teeth. *I want you to stop pointing that gun at me.*

With a coy smile, she flipped the gun and pointed it under her own chin. *Is that better?* she said.

No, he said, feeling panic bloom in his chest. *Please stop. Just give me the gun.*

She looked at his outstretched hands, then back at his face. She turned the gun so the handle was facing him, and handed it over.

He took the gun from her, exhaling in relief. He moved to put it in the back of his jeans, further from her reach.

No, she said. Her eyes were big and black and wet. He stopped.

Point it at me, she said.

His heart sank. He didn't move.

Point it at me, she said again.

Don't, he said.

She reached out and grabbed the waist of his jeans, pulling him toward her. *We're dead already*, she said. *Just point it at me.*

He raised the gun and pointed it at her face. She leaned forward and kissed him. Then she walked backward, toward the bed, pulling him with her by his belt.

She lay back on the bed, with him on top of her. The gun was in his right hand.

Keep it pointed at me, she said, and started to unfasten his belt. She released his cock, and hiked up her dress. She pulled him down toward her. He let the muzzle of the gun graze her temple. She slid his cock into her.

He thrust into her, not sure if he wanted it to be over or if he didn't want it to stop. His weight was on his elbows, with one hand in her hair and the other hand around his gun. All he could hear was the sound of flesh slapping against flesh.

She turned her head so she was facing the gun, and he instantly pulled it away.

Don't! she gasped.

He stopped. They were both panting. He was still inside of her. The gun was at his side.

She looked at him. He lifted the gun and pointed it at her face. She opened her mouth, and touched her tongue to the muzzle. He felt his cock stiffen harder inside her. Her tongue circled the muzzle. Then she opened her mouth wider and sucked the tip of it.

When she pulled away, the muzzle was shining wet.

Put it inside of me, she said.

He froze.

No, he said.

Please, she said.

I can't.

Please, she said again. She looked like she could cry.

It was far too late anyway.

He eased his cock out of her, then crouched down to her thighs. He wrapped his hand around the pistol's grip, keeping his fingers far from the trigger. Her knees were bent and her cunt glistened darkly.

He put the tip of the gun at her entrance, then slowly eased it inside of her. He heard her moan. He slowly pushed it further inside her, until the trigger guard pressed against her. Then he pulled it back and thrust it into her. Then again. And again.

Don't stop, she gasped. *Come here.*

He moved up so they were face to face, the gun still inside of her. He eased it back and forth. She moaned into his mouth as they kissed.

Then she pulled away and gently bit down on his earlobe.

Pull the trigger, she whispered.

He jerked his face back to look at her. She was staring back at him.

Jesus Christ! he cried. He pulled the gun out of her, too rough, then walked to the window, as far away from her as he could get.

His hands were shaking as he pulled back the pistol's slide and released the magazine, then put the magazine in his pocket. He redid his pants and belt. He holstered his weapon. His heart was beating wildly. He couldn't look at her.

Zain, she said in a hard voice. He didn't look at her. She sighed. He heard her moving around the room, gathering her things. He heard shoes on the motel room floor. Finally, he turned around. She'd pulled her dress back down and she was tottering on the high heels.

What are you doing? he said.

I'm going out, she said, then breezed past him and out the door.

At first, he was too angry to do anything except smoke and drink whiskey from the bottle. He hadn't wanted to hurt her. Why did she have to push him so hard that it became what he wanted?

Hours passed and worry started to eclipse his anger. Where was she? She'd gone out, alone, in the middle of the night, in that tiny dress and high heels she could barely walk in. She didn't even have her weapon with her.

He reloaded his gun and went out on the streets. He returned to the bar where they'd played pool, but she wasn't there. He returned to every other bar they'd been in. Nothing. He wandered the streets, passing laughing teenagers and old drunks, but there was no sight of a skinny girl with dyed hair and a frightening smile.

Finally, he returned to the hotel, hoping he'd find her there. But that hope flickered out when he opened the door to a dark and silent room.

He sat by the window, smoking.

If she comes back, he kept thinking, but couldn't finish the thought. *If she comes back...what?* Was he trying to bargain with a god he didn't believe in?

She had never pretended to be something she wasn't.

Finally, around four in the morning, the door opened and she came limping into the room. Her hair was a mess, eye makeup was streaked down her face, and there was an oval-shaped bruise forming along her jaw. She smelled like cigarettes and sex and tequila. She was barefoot.

She stood, staring at him.

Are you going to tell me what a shitty person I am? she said. Her voice was hoarse.

He looked at her. *No*, he said.

He handed her the bottle of whiskey. She took it from him and took a swig. He lit a second cigarette, then handed it to her.

If you want someone to beat the shit out of you, he said. *If you want someone to hit you or fuck you or put a hole in your head, then OK. But could you let it be me?*

She took a long drag of the cigarette, then exhaled.

You would do that? she asked.

Yes, he said.

Would you do that tonight?

His heart beat fast. Not tonight, he thought. *Yes*, he said.

She looked at him, and then walked to the bed. She pulled her dress up above her waist and lay down on her back. She wasn't wearing any underwear. There were bruises on her thighs and her recently-shaved pussy looked swollen and pink.

She let her legs fall open.

He put out his cigarette, then walked over to her. He took the cigarette from her hand and crushed it out. He climbed on top of her and unbuckled his pants. He stroked his cock hard and then eased it inside of her. She gasped in what sounded like pain.

Don't stop, she said.

He didn't.

• • • •

In the morning, he lay in bed and watched her get dressed. The bruise on her jaw had darkened to a deep purple and he saw there were more bruises—not only on her thighs, but on her wrists and arms too.

She sat on the bed and touched the bottom of her foot, which was scraped up, flecked with dried blood.

What happened to your shoes? he asked.

I don't know, she said. *Fuck high heels.*

Come here, he said. She crawled back to him, and he gathered her in his arms. Sometimes she felt so slight.

I'll kill you any time you want, he said. He didn't know if it was a joke or not.

Say it again, she said, in a muffled voice by his chest.

I'll kill you any time you want, he repeated, more softly.

She sighed and her body relaxed against his. He looked at the black line on her scalp. He felt such a tenderness for her. It was as if all the hardness he'd thought he'd built up over the years was just ice after all, easily melted.

Do you want to get some pie? he asked into her hair.

She pulled back and looked at him, her eyes bright. *Pie?* she said. *Can we?*

• • • •

They walked down the bright street to the nearby diner. But when they were a block away from the hotel she suddenly gasped and said, *My sunglasses!*

What?

My pink sunglasses!

Do you need them? Zain asked, but he could tell from the look on her face that there was no point arguing with her. They turned back.

Zain just happened to be looking at the man on the street at the exact moment the man noticed him turn around. The look on the man's face only changed for an instant, but Zain caught it. He felt his blood turn cold.

There were two men—one taller than the other, both white, both wearing sunglasses. They didn't speak to each other. They just kept walking as Zain and Reese walked toward them.

She looked over at him.

What is it? she said.

He gave her a false smile. *Nothing, honey*, he said.

He saw her face slacken. Then she pressed her lips together and smiled tightly back at him.

They kept their pace slow. They were getting closer to the two men. Zain and Reese were both carrying, of course, but he seriously doubted the men would start a shoot-out in the street. Charlie wouldn't have wanted that.

They passed the men, and kept walking. The hotel was in sight now. He didn't turn around. They had a better chance of escape if they men didn't realize they'd been made.

Hey, Zain said. *You wanna take a ride somewhere?*

Sure, she said.

Finally, they reached the hotel parking lot. *You drive,* he said, and handed her the keys. They got into the car.

Don't speed, don't do anything illegal, but get us out of here, he said.

She pulled out of the lot.

Any particular direction? she asked.

Just not south, he said. *We don't wanna get stopped at the border.*

She drove quickly, but without panic, heading north.

What is it? she said.

Two men. I've never seen them before today. One of them reacted when we turned around.

The guys with the sunglasses?

Yeah, he said.

Fuck.

Zain was watching in the rearview mirror when he saw the BMW appear, about a block away.

We might have a tail, he said. *Try and find out.*

She made a turn, and the BMW followed them. She made a second turn, and for several minutes there was no sight of the other car. She turned a third time, and then, in the distance, the BMW appeared again.

Lose them! he said.

She gunned it.

They tore down streets, through alleys, and around sudden turns. They would seem to lose the BMW and then it would appear, again and again. Finally, she made a frighteningly quick bolt across the railroad tracks, just before a train passed and cut off all traffic behind them.

She kept driving for another hour, taking odd twists and turns, until it was clear they were no longer being followed.

Then she looked over at him, and said, *You think I can pull over for a second?*

They were on a long narrow highway through ranchland. They could see any car approaching them from miles off, but there was no one else on the road.

Go ahead, he said.

She parked on the side of the road. She got out of the car, bent over, and threw up.

She spat a few times, then got back into the car, rolled down the window, and lit two cigarettes. She handed him one.

How long do you think they've been tailing us? she asked.

I don't know, he said. *Could be they tracked that first car, and have been on us since we arrived in Laredo. Or before then.*

They could have taken us out a hundred times. I haven't been looking out for anyone, she said.

He thought of them eating churros on the street, kissing in the alley. *Me neither,* he said. *So maybe they only just found us.* He sighed. *We have to figure out what to do next. I left my bag in the hotel, which had my passports and a stack of cash in it. We have the money in the spare tire, but that's about it. Your cash was in the room?*

Yeah, she said.

How many bullets are in your weapon?

Nine.

Good. Mine's loaded. We'll pick up more ammo as soon as we can.

So where to? she asked.

I'm thinking we head east, he said.

Why?

Well, we can't head south. We came from the north. And I don't want to head back toward LA.

She laughed. *So why not east?*

We can go to Florida, Miami maybe, he said. *We can pay to get onto a boat, and get out of the country, even without passports.*

OK, she said, *Let's go east.*

• • • •

It took all day just to get out of Texas. By the time they were in the middle of Louisiana, it was getting dark. Zain was driving and could feel her fidgeting.

Why don't you like driving at night? he asked.

I don't know, she said. *I guess I'm scared of the dark.*

He looked at her, thinking it was a joke, but she was still staring stonily out the window.

We should keep driving, he said, softly. Though they hadn't seen the BMW again, if the two men had decided to go east, it wouldn't be that hard for them to find Zain and Reese again.

I know, she said.

He drove through Louisiana, briefly through Alabama, and into Florida. The air became muggy and thick with the sound of humming cicadas.

He thought she would sleep, but she stayed awake, smoking and looking out at the darkness.

Finally, late into the night, he saw her head fall against the headrest. He reached over, took the lit cigarette from her hand, and tossed it out the open window.

His chest was heavy with dread. He felt that she'd been right—that they were somehow already marked for death.

He drove across Florida until he reached Jacksonville, then headed south. She woke up just as the sun started to rise.

Is it the ocean? she said. There was a body of sparkling blue water to their left.

It's a river, I think, that opens out to the ocean, he said.

Can we go to the ocean? Find a beach, I mean?

He had an image of her body, bleeding out onto the sand. He looked at her. Her hair was mussed and there was a long line running down her face from the car headrest. The bruise on her jaw was still a deep purple.

Sure, he said.

He drove to a state park, and then they walked through the dunes and across a narrow wooden walkway onto the beach. The sun was just starting to rise over the water, turning the sky yellow, then orange, then pink. The beach was flat and empty.

They walked toward the water. He stopped when his shoes started to sink into the wet sand, but she kept walking. She walked into the waves until the water was past her boots, then past her knees, then past her waist. Then she dove in and disappeared.

He felt strangely calm.

She emerged laughing, soaking wet. She ran up the beach, then collapsed onto the dry sand. He lay down next to her, and lit them a couple of cigarettes. They lay on their backs. There were still a few faint stars in the sky.

Zain Vincent Solano, she said.

He looked at her. She was still staring at the sky. *You looked through my bag*, he said.

I did.

I should've known.

Two passports, she said. *One in your real name and one under an alias. All those nice clothes. A little black toiletries kit. A key chain with five keys on it. And a roll of cash. Are you sorry you lost it all?*

No, he said. *We could've used the cash, but with one passport in my name and one under the alias Charlie created, it's probably better I didn't use either.*

What about all your stuff in LA? Your place, the food in your fridge, the people who might be missing you? You ever think about that?

Sometimes, he said. *But the truth is, very few people will even notice I'm gone. I didn't make much impact on the world.*

Maybe, she said. She raised herself onto her elbows and looked down at him. *But not none.*

No, he said. *Not none.*

He brushed away the drops of seawater that had collected on her eyebrows and cheeks. She kissed him. She tasted like salt.

They walked back to the parking lot, and stopped at the public restroom, a small weather-beaten shack with a women's entrance on one side and a men's entrance on the other. He went right and she went left.

When he walked out, he saw a flash of movement, and barely had time to duck before he heard a bullet explode into the wall behind where his head had just been.

He dove back into the restroom, then backed against the wall and drew his gun.

No one came in after him. Why should they, when they had him cornered?

He considered. There was most likely a man at each restroom entrance. They could wait as long as they liked. But then again, one might decide to storm his way in—to the men's restroom, or the women's. Or she might decide to get things moving a little more quickly. And what would he do—hide in a bathroom while they gunned her down?

He thought of something Charlie had once told him. *If you're caught in a real tight spot, your one hope is to come out shooting. Audacity and dumb luck are the only things that might save you.*

So be it.

He came out shooting.

He saw the man, saw the gun pointed at him, and heard his own weapon discharging before he heard the sound of another pistol, and he knew he had fired first, knew even as his shoulder was knocked back by a searing heat. He watched the man in front of him fall, then looked to the man behind him, who was firing his weapon. There was another searing pain, this time to his gut, but Zain had a clear shot to the second man's head and he squeezed the trigger and then that man fell too.

He stepped toward the women's room but there was a sudden movement from the parking lot. A car door opening. It wasn't the BMW, and all Zain could do was pray it wasn't some bystander as he aimed his weapon and shot the windshield once, twice, and a cloud of blood bloomed across the shattered glass.

He ran to the car and in the front seat was a body, the head all a mess, a pistol in its hands. No one else in the car.

That meant there had been two cars. Three men. Unless-

He turned back, but it was already too late. The fourth man had come from around the restroom and was walking toward him. Zain lifted his weapon, but the man already had a pistol aimed right at him. Zain looked at the man's face. He knew.

I was washing my hands when I heard the sound of a gun being fired through a noise suppressor. I froze. After a minute, I heard the sound of many shots being fired, both with and without a suppressor. I withdrew my weapon. Two more shots came, along with the sound of breaking glass. My jacket was still wet and I realized my gun had been soaked by my swim in the ocean. Would it still fire? I'd find out soon.

As I whipped around the corner, I heard another shot ring out. There were two bodies bleeding out in front of the bathroom.

Someone moved in the parking lot. I saw a man walking away from me, his gun drawn. He was looking down. I ran toward the parking lot.

The man was looking down at a body. The man was looking down at Zain's body. He turned as I approached and I shot without aiming. He fell.

I ran to Zain. There was a bullet hole in the center of his forehead. His eyes were open wide. I crouched down and touched his lips with my finger. They were still warm. I leaned over and kissed him.

Then I heard a groaning sound. The man I had just shot was still alive.

I aimed my gun at his head, then stopped, considering.

I tore the laces out of my boots and approached the man. I had shot him in the side, I saw now. He was covered in blood but still very much alive. I kicked him over, onto his stomach, then grabbed both his wrists. I tied his hands together, tightly. Then I dragged him over to our car, and, after several tries, managed to get him in the trunk. I slammed the door shut.

I walked back to Zain. I knelt next to him and closed his eyes. My fingers traced blood down his face.

. . . .

I had thought I wasn't good at extracting information from people. It turned out I had simply been lacking the necessary motivation.

After several hours of driving, I located an abandoned boathouse, and dragged the man out of the trunk and into it. I didn't have the creativity for torture, but using my gun as a club turned out to be plenty effective. It didn't take long for the man to tell me how they'd found us—they'd put a small tracking device on the car.

He resisted telling me anything about Charlie, but after a few hours, I got the information I needed from him. An address. It was enough.

I left the man's body in a bloody heap, a bullet in his head.

• • • •

I removed the tracking device from the car, then drove for two days straight. I reached Los Angeles in the middle of the night. I ditched the car in a deserted part of town, then walked for a few miles until I reached a shitty little hotel that I'd never been to and where Charlie would never think to look for me.

I stepped into a small room with a creaky bed and an old television set. There was no bathroom in the room, just a shared toilet down the hall.

I lit a cigarette. I thought of the steady flame of Zain's Zippo. I wished I had taken something of his. There had been nothing in the car worth keeping, except the cash, which I had left hidden in the spare tire. I had nothing but the clothes I wore, my weapon, and a wallet with about $200 cash in it.

I wished I had something to prove that that man had thought I was something more than nothing. Not just something he owned, like his lighter, but a piece of him. A cutting of his hair, maybe. No, I wanted to see his face again. No. I wanted him to be here, alive, just for one more moment. Or forever, instead of me.

I put out the cigarette. I got into the bed and cried until I fell asleep.

· · · ·

In the morning, I stole a car off the street—a Toyota Corolla—and drove to the address I'd gotten off of Charlie's man. It wasn't Charlie's home, of course, but it was a safehouse in the valley the guy said Charlie visited often.

I didn't have to wait long. Charlie drove up by himself, in a gray Lexus GX. The gate opened and he disappeared inside.

I was prepared to wait for hours, but after a few minutes, the gate reopened, and Charlie's car emerged. I followed him from the house, making sure to keep my distance. I followed him through Bel Air, into Beverly Hills. He pulled up in front of an elegant looking hotel, where he got out of his car and handed his keys to the valet.

I parked my stolen car in front of a fire hydrant, then walked away from it, into the hotel.

I stepped into a large lobby with a glittering chandelier, huge vases of flowers, and Rococo-style furniture. I walked through the lobby, peering into the bar and the various sitting rooms, but didn't see him. I walked through the restaurant to the outside patio, which had wrought iron furniture with white tabletops, white umbrellas, and a white wooden fence all around it. I was just considering how the hell I'd be able to track him down if he was in one of the hotel rooms, when I saw Charlie's profile. He was sitting at one of the tables, alone.

I slowly withdrew my gun from its holster, but held it low. I walked toward him.

Charlie looked up when I got closer. He was wearing a green and white striped polo shirt. He looked the same as he always did. He smiled but didn't move.

Reese, he said, *Won't you sit down?*

Of course, he should have been dead already. If I'd done what he'd taught me.

I sat in the chair across from him. He was leaning back, his hands clasped on the table in front of him. Underneath the table, I pointed my gun at him. It was, of course, the Glock 17 he'd given me as a present.

How ya doing, kid? he said.

Whatever steeliness I had felt seemed to melt away. I felt a rush of affection for Charlie, and a familiar desire to please him. This was an instinct I didn't have to act on, I reminded myself. But I had no doubt that Charlie sensed it.

You sent four men after me, I said.

Five, actually, he said.

And just like that, I iced over again. Charlie may have just been doing what he got paid to do, but it didn't mean he didn't deserve to die.

Zain was one of my best guys, you know, he said. *I chose him specially for this job. He was always a professional. I figured no matter what weird shit he saw you get into, and no matter how pathetic or cracked up you might seem, he'd go through with it. But he didn't. Why not?*

I shrugged. *He was tired of the job*, I said. *He didn't want to do it anymore.*

Uh-huh. Look, I can believe he was tired of the job. Lots of people get tired of the job. But they don't suddenly give up in the middle of a hit and try and flee to Mexico with their mark. Zain worked for me for eight years. Six days of following you and he threw that all away.

That was his choice, I said.

Come on. This had nothing to do with you?

I knew Charlie was trying to distract me from the business at hand. I knew I should shoot him and get it done with. But the chance to talk about Zain had a pull on me I couldn't resist.

I didn't tell him not to kill me. In fact, I told him he should, more than once, I said.

And yet there's something about you. You don't even know it, do you? You're such a goddamn mess that it makes people want to try and piece you back together. Even I thought I could, once. But it's pointless, isn't it? You'll never be a complete person. Zain had a whole life ahead of him.

Suddenly I found I couldn't swallow. *You think I don't know that? I* said. *But I can't undo what I did.* I felt myself harden again, and added, *And neither can you.*

Charlie just looked at me levelly.

So what are you gonna do, kid? Eliminate me, get out of this line of work, and then what? What's your plan, exactly?

I shrugged. *I don't have a plan*, I said. *But it doesn't matter. Something's different in me.*

Is it? he said. *Or is that just what you want to believe?*

Suddenly, I was tired of Charlie. He was stalling.

You know, Charlie, I said. *I always thought you knew everything. But now-*

Suddenly, Charlie reached into his coat. I pulled the trigger and shot him in the crotch. I stood up over him. He was gasping for breath. I aimed at his heart, and fired the gun again.

I looked down at him. I thought about finishing my sentence, like they would in a movie. But I didn't.

I walked past the tables of screaming people, out a back entrance. I walked down an alley that was lined with white delivery trucks.

The sun was high in the sky, shining brightly down on me, purifying everything it touched.

• • • •

THE END

About the Author

Rachel Tusler is a fiction writer and playwright from the United States. In 2022 and 2023, Tusler had short stories published in Eunoia Review. *The Killing Machine* is her first novella.

As a librettist and lyricist, Tusler has created two musicals with composer Rory Stitt: *Shanghaied!* and *The Moment*, which have been workshopped in Portland, Oregon and Bangkok, Thailand. Tusler is an enrolled member of the Osage Nation of Oklahoma.